Julie Bozza

Butterfly Hunter

LIBRAtiger

Published by LIBRAtiger 2018

ISBN: 978-1-925869-22-4

First published by Manifold Press 2012

Text: © Julie Bozza 2018
Proof–reading and line editing: F.M. Parkinson
Editor: Fiona Pickles of Manifold Press
Print format: © Julie Bozza 2018
Set in Adobe Caslon and Adobe Gothic

Cover design: © Gayna Murphy of Mubu Design | mubudesign.com

libra-tiger.com | juliebozza.com

Acknowledgements

With love to my stalwart technical advisor, Mr B.

With thanks to the person whose comment on Goodreads unknowingly inspired this novel.

With love to Pete Murray for his honest, emotional songwriting and his passionate performances.

And with gratitude in anticipation of the reader's tolerance. I wrote some of this story conscious that I am an outsider looking in at things some will say don't concern me. I did so with nothing in my heart but a love of and a wish for interdependence between all our peoples – and for that perhaps any infelicities will be forgiven.

one

Dave Taylor looked down at the perfect little human creature he held cradled in his hands – delicate skin, warm scent, fragile bones – and asked, "Tell me again why she isn't ours?"

Over at the kitchen bench, Denise snorted, her hands busily assembling their lunch. "You know why, Davey."

"I still haven't found what I'm looking for?" he hazarded.

"See? I knew you'd listen eventually."

"I didn't know that I even *had* to look …" Dave gazed down at this exquisite tiny replica of Denise, and let out a sigh, wondering why she was so sure he wasn't looking for this, exactly this. They had been Denny-and-Davey for so very long, since his very first day at school over twenty years ago, and it bewildered him why they weren't Denny-and-Davey-and-Zoe now. The baby's fine hair glowed golden, as his own and Denise's did; Zoe didn't even have any of her father's dark Italian looks, at least not from what Dave could make out.

"Hey," he murmured a greeting as the baby's eyes fluttered a little and then opened to return his gaze with solemn blue. "Hey there, Zo. I'm Davey." The baby turned to curl trustingly into his chest. "I'm your … Well. I'm your mum's best mate. I think."

"Course you are," Denise put in with brisk scorn for the notion that there could be any doubt about it. There was a brief scowl of frustration from Zoe, and then a yawn which threatened to become a wail. Denise came over and put a plate of sandwiches down on the table before Dave, and then took Zoe, settled in a chair round the corner and rearranged her own clothing so that Zoe could feed. Denise's very matter-of-factness emphasised that Dave was considered as mostly harmless now; not even the ex, but only the friend who had no chance at all of regathering what he'd lost.

"Where's Vittorio?" he asked, reaching for a sandwich, and keeping his eyes politely averted – as if he hadn't known that very breast as intimately as anyone might, not so long ago.

"Work. He got called out; he'll be a while." Denise paused to shift Zoe a little in her arms, as if still trying to find the right hold. The baby wasn't even two weeks old. "What did you want to talk about? You said you had a trip coming up?"

"Yeah. I could be gone for a while. It's all happened very quickly."

"That's good," she replied – then added as if bracing him up, "It's good for business. Tour group, is it?"

"No, just one guy. An English earl, for God's sake! Well, the son of an earl, or something. I've been dealing with the father's butler, and he wasn't real specific. What does that make him? The son, I mean."

"Out of place. Out of time! What's he doing over here?"

Dave groaned. "Chasing down some mythical butterfly. Apparently no one's even sure it ever existed in the first place."

"A quest!" Denise's eyes had lit up, though Dave knew well enough it was at least half in humour. "A knight on a quest! A *genuine* knight!"

"Um, yeah, so –"

"And you're his squire!"

"Oh God, shut up, would you?" he grumbled good–naturedly. "It's just as well that Japanese tour group cancelled for June. He's booked me for three months."

That sobered her up. "You're gonna be out there for *three months*?"

Dave essayed a shrug. "Not the whole time, of course. But the idea is that we get this done, whatever it takes. When I told them I had that week's trip in July with the Americans, he said he'd come along, too, if he was welcome, or he'd wait for me to meet up with him again afterwards. And if we find the damned butterflies early, he's paying me the full fee anyway."

"Huh," was her only response. A thoughtful silence stretched while Zoe finished up on one breast and was switched to the other. Dave stared out the French windows at the backyard until Denise was decently rearranged.

"I just don't know what to expect," Dave said.

"Why? Not cos he's English. Your dad was English!"

"Yeah, I always forget that." Dave smiled a bit wistfully. He still missed his dad. "But that's not it."

"What's the problem, then?"

"I only hope he's up to it. The guy who made the booking – his butler or secretary or whatever – he said –"

"What?"

"Just before he hung up, he said – Well. To treat him kindly. So I'm left thinking God knows *what* to expect."

"He didn't tell you why?"

"Nope. And I even asked; I followed up with an email. He just shrugged me off, all very proper and dignified, as if he hadn't even said it in the first place."

"Huh." Eventually Denise asked, "So where do you start, when you're looking for a butterfly that may or may not even exist?"

"The other side of Cunnamulla. There's supposed to be a waterhole – though it's not on any maps – and that's –"

"A *mythical* waterhole?"

"Pretty much straight out of Dreamtime. Yeah."

"You'll need to talk to Charlie, won't you?" Denise visibly relaxed at the notion. "You talk to Charlie before you head out there, and you take care, do you hear me, Davey? *You take care.*"

"Course I will," he scoffed. "How many years have I been doing this?"

"No, I mean it. You have to come back, see, cos you're gonna be – well, whatever the irreligious version of a godparent is, for Zoe."

An irreligious godparent … ? Dave just laughed. But before he left he pressed a gentle kiss to the top of Zoe's milk–scented golden–haired head, and he silently wished her well. Just in case.

The plane was due in just after seven in the morning. Dave made sure he was there in plenty of time, even though the Englishman would need to go through passport control, collect his luggage, and then get through quarantine. All of which would take an hour, probably – but it would be just Dave's luck if he turned up at eight to find that the earl's son had been processed as a VIP or some such thing, and had been waiting on him ever since.

Dave found a place to lean on the waist–high barriers with the drivers and others carrying signs. His own read *GORING*. That was the guy's name. Nicholas Goring. Which perhaps made his father Earl Goring, or was it the Earl of Goring … ? When Dave wasn't chatting in an early morning haze to his current companions, he spent the time trying to remember whether he'd had any clue about whether Nicholas was the eldest son or not – and if he was, whether that meant Dave should address him as 'my lord' or as 'sir'.

He'd looked it up on Wikipedia, realised he'd need to email the butler for more information, and then promptly let it all slip his mind.

He was kicking himself, metaphorically at least. He was always more professional than this. Always. And all right, maybe titles didn't matter very much – though he was sure they'd matter more to an Englishman than an Australian – but no one could afford to be this slapdash in the Outback. Why would Goring trust Dave with his life, if he couldn't even get this detail right?

Dave sighed, and watched in a desultory way as the passengers from other flights straggled through. No one looked their best after a 24-hour flight. No one. This pair now, for instance – a father and a young daughter, Dave assumed – appeared beyond tired, irritable, dishevelled, unhappy. That all fell away, however, as they were greeted by an older couple. The man's parents, the girl's grandparents: they had to be. Faces brightened, postures lifted, hugs all round.

It would take a miracle to perform the same transformation on the next pair who came through the gates, though. A married couple, perhaps, whose marriage didn't look like it would survive the rigours of an international flight. Dave and Denny had done that once, of course – headed off on the obligatory backpacking holiday in their late teens. They'd done all right together, despite having laughably little money and even less sense. But then, they'd always been friends first, and a best mate could see you through anything. They'd taken turns seeing each other through.

Dave tried not to sigh again, and then tried not to yawn, as he absently watched the next fellow come through. The luggage came first, on a trolley, and the guy came after it, almost tumbling as he negotiated the doors and got a foot caught against the trolley wheel. Everything teetered as he tried to break free, prevent the door from slamming closed, and head down along the barriers to his right, all at the same time. He almost succeeded in achieving all those things, and probably would have, too, if he hadn't suddenly decided to head to his left instead. He went sprawling on the floor, long limbs everywhere, while the trolley trundled off by itself for a few feet and finally came to an unconvincing kind of halt.

Dave felt for the guy, he really did. Just his luck if he was meeting his lover at the airport or something, and had managed to gawk out entirely. Everyone was either tactfully looking somewhere else, or smiling ruefully at the guy. There wasn't anyone nearby to help him up, because none of them were dumb enough to go past the barrier; security didn't seem to have noticed yet, and for now the blunderer was the only arriving passenger.

And he was still lying there on the floor ... Why on earth was he still down there on the cold hard floor? He hadn't broken something, had he? Dave looked at him – properly – with a frown. Considered each of those gangly limbs, but they seemed to be whole. He wasn't lying at an awkward angle or anything. But his head was tilted back, and he was grinning a bit stupidly ... and he was looking right back at Dave!

Which would have been fine, except that once he realised Dave was looking back, the guy seemed to wink. Or was that blink? But upside down like that, his smile seemed to have a wicked kick to it – and really, if they were in any other situation at all, if this wasn't early morning at an international airport, Dave might have thought the guy was checking him out ...

He turned away with a bit of a grimace, kind of a sneer. Which wasn't like him, not really, and he wasn't prejudiced, he'd swear it, but honestly it was *way* too early for lascivious stares from awkward strangers of the wrong gender. It just was.

A moment later he regretted the rudeness, of course, and his heart thudded once, punishingly. He turned back to see if he'd given offence, and perhaps to offer an apologetic shrug. But security had finally arrived, and were helping the guy up to his feet, dusting him off, making sure he would remain upright for now, retrieving his bags. Listening to him chat, and apparently letting themselves be charmed into considering him harmless.

Dave watched, vaguely glad that everything seemed to be in order. Until they were past the barriers, and the guards ushered the guy out towards the exits, and he declined to go. Instead he turned, and his searching gaze soon landed on Dave again. Dave stood up slowly, warily, as the man approached with the guards trailing behind with matching frowns.

"I believe you're looking for me," the guy said in a cultured English accent.

"What?" Dave replied stupidly.

A long pale hand indicated the sign Dave carried. "I'm Nicholas Goring."

"Oh God."

The corner of his mouth kicked slightly, though the man was no longer smiling. "Just *sir* will do."

They were silent while Dave led his client out to the car park, paid off his ticket, found the car and put the bags in the boot, insisting in a mutter that he didn't need Goring's assistance.

It wasn't until they were heading into the city on Kingsford Smith Drive that Dave finally spoke. "I'll take you to the hotel. I booked it with an early check–in. I'm sure you'll be glad of a shower and change of clothes." When he risked a glance at the man, Dave was disconcerted to find that Goring's smile once again had a wicked kick to it. "Um," said Dave, "*sir* …"

"I always had a thing for chauffeurs," the man confided.

"Huh." Dave frowned, and stared very hard at the road ahead, though he wasn't entirely sure how much he was actually seeing. "Well. What do you do when they don't have a thing for you?"

Goring chuckled, sounding genuinely amused. "Ah, come on. Seize the day!"

"Mate, life's not *that* short."

The chuckle turned into a laugh – and Dave liked that. Still, he was relieved when Goring said, "All right, I'll stop. Don't mind me. I hardly got a wink of sleep on that damned plane."

"You weren't exactly travelling cattle class. Were you?"

"No, but …" Goring looked away, biting at his lower lip. He was a tall, scrawny man, and his lips were the plumpest thing about him. They were a dash of pink on his pale face. They were almost pretty. "Too much on my mind, I suppose."

Dave let a beat go by, and then headed for safer ground. "Common wisdom is to stay awake for as long as you can today, and try not to sleep until tonight. Get into the new time zone as soon as you can."

"Yes, so I've heard."

"And I find that people like to start with a good breakfast, to keep their energy levels up. The hotel – you're at the Hilton – is known for their breakfasts."

"I see."

"It's up to you, but I'll keep you company, if you like. For as much of the day as suits."

"Starting with breakfast … ?"

"If you like," Dave repeated. "And later, if you have people here, I can drop you off wherever. Just tell me what you want to do and then, you know, feel free to change your plans if you can't stay awake any longer or whatever."

Goring was staring at him. "I understand." After a moment, he added, "I don't know why I was expecting laconic rather than loquacious."

Dave glanced at him. "Dunno if I'm your typical Aussie, mate."

Another laugh, though wry this time rather than genuine. Then Goring asked, "Will Mr Taylor be able to join us for breakfast?"

"What?" Dave grimaced as he turned right onto Albert Street. They were almost there. "No, I'm – *I'm* Dave Taylor."

"Oh."

"I guess I didn't – No, I didn't introduce myself. The meeting at the airport didn't, uh –"

"Didn't quite go as planned," Goring smoothly supplied.

"No. My fault. Look, we're here," Dave said. "I'll drop you off, and you can check in while I park."

"No need. I'll stay with you."

Dave glanced at him, and thought that Goring wasn't merely being polite. In any case, he needed to decide right away, as he was already approaching the car park. He nodded, and flipped on the indicator. So be it. Almost nothing this morning had gone as intended, so why not this as well?

They were silent again as Dave collected a ticket, and then quickly chose an empty space on the ground floor – it was still too early to be busy. Once he'd parked, they both got out, and met around the back of the car. Dave looked the man in the eye, and held his hand out. "Good morning, uh, sir. I'm Dave Taylor."

Goring shook his hand with a cool firmness before disengaging. "I'm pleased to meet you, Mr Taylor. Call me Nicholas."

"Dave."

"David," said Nicholas.

Dave grinned, and turned to open the boot, started lifting the three bags out. "All right, but no one calls me that. It's Dave or – well, my friends call me Davey."

"Would you join me for breakfast, David?"

"Sure. Thanks," he added, quite genuinely. "We can talk over your trip. I've brought maps and such."

"Good. Here, let me –"

But Dave only handed over the cabin–sized bag, and insisted on wheeling the larger cases. "I've got it," he said. He attempted the three syllables as they emerged into sunlight: "Nicholas." He wondered how long it would be before he was allowed to go with Nick or Nicky.

"Thank you." The man's smile was a little gentler by now.

Of course it had all gone horribly wrong so far, and God only knew what that meant for the rest of the trip, but it seemed that at least Dave had been forgiven for his part of the shambles. He nodded, both accepting and returning the thanks. Nicholas seemed to understand. As they walked shoulder to shoulder into the hotel, Dave dared to think the next three months mightn't be a complete disaster.

Barely half an hour later, Nicholas reappeared, bright and fresh and cheerful in the diffuse sunlight of the restaurant. While still standing there towering tall and lean, he offered, "I apologise for the chauffeur thing."

Dave couldn't help but grin. "You're sorry about your thing for chauffeurs?"

"Well, no," was the reply as Nicholas sat down around the corner of the table to Dave's right. "That dates back to my first love. Always a formative experience, wouldn't you say?"

Dave huffed an empathic breath. "Hell, yeah."

"What I'm sorry for is being so outrageous so early in the morning with no provocation on your part whatsoever."

"Don't worry about it. We already started over, didn't we?"

"With our proper introductions," Nicholas agreed.

A waiter appeared, and Dave ordered coffee while Nicholas ordered tea.

Perhaps it was all best forgotten about, but Dave was still curious about the misunderstandings. "You know, I always do this bit. Meeting my clients off the plane, or whatever. To me, that's the professional thing to do. Maybe you're used to butlers and maids and secretaries – and chauffeurs," he added, as he caught Nicholas trying to suppress a wicked smirk – "doing that for you, but here there's just me. The business is mine, and I try to do things properly." Having forgotten the point he was trying to get to, Dave tailed off, "Well, I wouldn't just send a car to collect you."

"Of course not," Nicholas stoutly agreed. "It was my mistake entirely."

For some reason, Dave felt the need to persist. "There are a few people I employ to help me when I have larger tour groups, but for smaller groups – and for you – I'm afraid it's just me."

"That's perfectly fine. Of course."

A silence stretched. Dave frowned, unable to either follow his own thought processes through to their outcome, or track them back to their origin.

"Look," said Nicholas after their tea and coffee had arrived. "I won't flirt. I won't make a nuisance of myself. If that's what you're worried about. What I said this morning was stupid. But if an apology and a promise aren't enough, then –"

"That's enough," Dave insisted. But then he blurted, "The chauffeur. What happened to him?"

Nicholas's head went back in surprise. "Oh. Well. He went on to lead a full and happy life, I suppose. What do you mean, what happened … ?"

"He lost his job, right? Sacked without a reference?"

"Good grief," Nicholas exclaimed with a laugh. "Even I don't characterise my life as a Gothic romance. No, he didn't lose his job. Quite the opposite. He retired last May, and still lives on the estate."

Dave stared at the man.

"He was very kind to me," Nicholas continued. "Very patient. And," he confided from under a lifted brow, "very discreet."

"Oh!" Dave hadn't felt so idiotic for years.

"So, you see … it isn't *always* an unmitigated disaster to be fancied by me."

"No. No, of course …"

"Shall we go raid the buffet for breakfast?" Nicholas smoothly supplied.

Once they were done eating, they ordered more coffee and tea, and Dave reached for his folder of maps and notes. "Can we talk about the trip?"

"Yes, please." Nicholas sat forward with an eager little smile, his hands spread on the table either side of his cup.

"Look," said Dave after a long moment.

Nicholas's face fell. "There's a problem?"

"I just don't want you getting your hopes up, is all. The information you gave me – a lot of it's contradictory, or it doesn't make much sense."

"I know it's only clues. That's why I was hoping we'd have plenty of time to explore. Maybe it will all start falling into place while we're out there."

"That's the thing. And I tried having this conversation with your butler or whatever he was, so I'm hoping he passed all this on. Heading into the Outback – it's not like taking a stroll through the Cotswolds or whatever. If things go wrong, we could die."

"I understand," Nicholas solemnly replied.

"So we really need a better plan than just wandering about at random, hoping the clues will add up. If they even *are* clues."

"I understand, I really do. And I'm prepared for it all coming to naught. I know I might get nothing more from this than a rather peculiar holiday."

Dave grinned despite himself. "You don't seem the type to give up, though."

"No. I'd hope to come back next year, and try again. With you, if you can stand it; with someone else, if you can't."

"All right," said Dave. "I'm glad you said that about having plenty of time. You realise we're not going to be leaving Brisbane right away? There are still things to organise. And if we're heading north, the Wet's really only just ended – the wet season. It ran quite late this year. There's no point in hurrying."

"From what I understand of the geography, I don't think we'll be heading that far north."

"Aren't butterflies generally a tropical creature?"

"Not these ones." Nicholas's fingers skittered against the edge of the table, as if he wanted to drum impatiently but was too polite. "When will we leave, do you think?"

"A few days at least. Maybe a week. We need to plan exactly where we're going, and if we're going to be leaving the established roads, then we need to ask permission of whoever owns the land."

"Is that likely to be a problem?"

"I shouldn't think so; if the owners don't already know me, they'll know people who'll vouch for me. But it's only fair to ask before rather than after, if we can."

"Of course. I understand."

"Then it's a fair drive, just to get to Cunnamulla. So I'll leave one day, and you fly out the next, and I'll … collect you from the airport. Again."

Nicholas's smile was quirking irrepressibly.

"Or I'll send a driver to fetch you and bring you to the hotel, maybe. If you're lucky."

"No, I'd rather it was you," Nicholas said with a little more warmth than might be expected. "And anyway," he continued with a rather cooler directness, "I'd rather stay with you. I'd rather you drove me. Unless there's some particular reason why not."

"It's a long way, and there's not much to see. You'll get bored."

Nicholas shrugged. "I'd rather experience it. I'd rather … get a feel for the country."

"You have no idea about the distances involved. I mean, you can drive across England in an afternoon, can't you?"

"All the more reason to, um … broaden my horizons." The man really had the most infectious grin.

"Well –"

"It's like watching cricket," Nicholas said, overriding any protest that Dave had been about to make. "You're an Australian, you should know about cricket."

Dave made a noise tentatively indicating agreement and conveying an unwillingness to get into an argument over such a contentious issue just now.

"It's like watching a Test match. It might get a bit tedious on occasion, watching the full game. But you get a sense of it unfolding that way. You get a real feel for how the game is playing out. You never get that from watching the highlights."

Dave laughed, and surrendered. "Well, I can't argue with a cricket analogy."

"My best guess," said Nicholas, peering down at the state map and circling a region with a fingertip, "is that we start around here." He had long pale fingers; they were, perhaps, the most elegant thing about him. Dave watched as they traced lightly across the map as if the man could feel the land's contours. "Yes … and then we head further west, if we don't find anything there." After another long moment passed, Nicholas looked up. "What do you think?"

Dave shook himself out of his silence. "Area the size of Wales," he remarked.

"Yes. I realise it's a needle in a haystack and all that, but I have to *try*. This might be the only thing I –"

When the conclusion wasn't forthcoming, Dave prompted, "The only thing you what?"

Nicholas's gaze remained fixed on the map. "Never mind."

Dave let a moment go by, and then got the conversation back on track. "Okay, take me through the logic of it again. You started with a settler's journal."

"Yes. Clemence Hall. She's not very well known."

"And she mentioned a blue cloud."

Nicholas nodded enthusiastically. "They were travelling south–west from the Wyandra region, taking it slowly. This blue cloud would appear near the horizon each afternoon. She thought it was a mirage, but it stayed in the same location while their expedition continued on south. She wanted to go investigate, but one of the party was quite ill, and they didn't have enough water to take another detour." Nicholas's eyes were afire with the possibilities. "And I thought, what could that blue cloud be, but butterflies rising in the afternoon sunshine?"

"All right," Dave said. "But then didn't she say something about being north of the stone–curlew? If she meant Quilpie, then they weren't travelling south–west from Wyandra. Quilpie's to the north."

"I think she was referring to a Dreamtime site, not a settlers' town."

"Oh. Of course." Dave felt supremely idiotic. Imagine a Pom making that leap before a dinky–di Aussie …

Nicholas spared him a sympathetic look. "I've been obsessing over this for a while, you know."

"So I guess you did your research about possible sacred sites? Your butler or whatever didn't mention anything to do with the Dreamtime."

"I haven't found anything in the Dreamtime stories about the stone–curlew, or not yet anyway … but I did find a story about the Barcoo grunter – Great name, by the way."

"The fish … ?" Dave clarified, having to make yet another leap. "What's that got to do with curlews?"

"Yes, the *Scortum barcoo*. And the connection is with the butterflies."

"Right …" he prompted, feeling rather bewildered.

"The story ended with the Barcoo grunter ancestor returning to his long sleep, sinking deep *deep* down into his waterhole, and pieces of the sky – this is a loose translation, I admit – rose up to lament and flutter in farewell."

"But …"

"He was farewelling his love," Nicholas supplied, "who lived in the sky."

"Your butterflies were, like, the Barcoo grunter's tears?"

"Yes."

"Have you *seen* a grunter? They're ugly things."

Nicholas sat back with a disapproving sniff. "Even ugly creatures feel love, you know. Even ugly creatures can create beauty."

"Of course. I –" Dave hardly knew what to say. This contradictory Englishman had taken that personally, which meant that he must count himself among the ugly creatures of this world, when it was surely blindingly obvious to anyone with eyes that … Well. Dave wasn't about to tell some guy he'd just met – or indeed *any* guy – that he was beautiful. Nicholas Goring was strange, perhaps, yet undeniably beautiful with his long face and longer fingers, his deep blue gaze and his wicked smile, and the way he lit up when he talked about his mythical blue butterflies …

And what was Dave even doing, thinking things like that? About a *bloke?* "All right," Dave said, his voice unaccountably rough. "So we need to find out about sacred sites for stone–curlews and Barcoo grunters, if we can. I know just who to talk to. I'll call ahead, but if he's home then we're heading for Charleville first. As long as the sites aren't off–limits. There might be secret elements to the story that –"

"You think I don't know that? Of course I'd respect that."

Dave let the matter drop for now. That was the first sign of irritability from a man who'd survived a hellish twenty–four hours on a plane. Dave himself wouldn't have gone half so long without snapping.

"If you're in the mood for a walk," Dave offered, "the city botanic gardens are about ten minutes away, on a bend of the river. They're pretty cool. And they date back to convict days, so they're historical as well."

Nicholas considered him for a moment, and then said rather remotely,

"All right."

"Stretch your legs. Get some fresh air."

A reluctant smile tweaked the corner of Nicholas's mouth. "Don't humour me."

"Is that what I was doing?" Dave asked with mock innocence. "Well, what d'you say to a stroll around the gardens?"

The smile was small but genuine by now. "I say yes."

Dave watched as Nicholas ambled along, hands snagged in his jeans pockets and long face turned towards the sun, long eyelashes fanning darkly down over his cheekbones. In the strong light, the Englishman appeared beyond pale – almost translucent, like the fine china Dave's grandmother used to treasure. So pale and fine, but with an odd tinge of cool colour, as well. Nicholas looked as if he'd been raised in the shade all his life. God only knew how he'd cope with the harsh realities of Australia.

"You know about protection, right?" Dave asked.

Nicholas tilted his head to quirk a suggestive eyebrow at Dave.

"*Sun* protection," Dave clarified.

"Heavens, can't I soak in a bit of warmth – just for a few minutes?"

"Yeah, but *only* for a few minutes." Dave added, "I'm going to buy you a hat."

Nicholas laughed. "You assume I don't have one? Or that it's inadequate?"

"Well –"

"You think I came out here equipped with my grandfather's old pith helmet, do you?"

"Mate, I am going to buy you a genuine Akubra."

The man's expression turned fondly droll. Or drolly fond. Whichever was worse for Dave's peace of mind. But all Nicholas said was a soft "Thank you."

The two of them wandered on quietly for a while, until they reached the river, and turned to follow along the bank. Well, Dave turned – and then he had to reach back and snag Nicholas by the elbow and turn him before he walked off the path and right into the water, he was so busy gazing up at the trees and the sky.

"Mate, you've got to look where you're going," Dave advised.

Nicholas murmured something appreciative, and continued on with his head metaphorically in the wide blue expanse above.

"Okay," Dave announced, "it's time for The Talk."

"Oh dear!" said Nicholas, though he didn't sound very worried.

"I've let you talk me into a few things today, but you've got to understand that when we're out there, what I say goes. I make the rules, I make the decisions, I get the last word. Every time. Do you understand?"

Nicholas pulled a long face. "Well –"

"No quibbles, no arguments, no second–guessing. This isn't a democracy."

"The whole point of this is to find the butterflies."

"I'll find your butterflies for you, if we possibly can. But that's only ever our second priority, all right? Our first is to return home, safe and whole. Those are my priorities, and those are going to be your priorities, too."

Nicholas immediately brightened. "Oh, if that's all –"

"No, that's not *all*."

"What else, then?"

"I mean, you can't just dismiss it like that. This is serious. There aren't many places left in the world where your survival depends on you alone, but this is one of them. And your survival depends on you and on me."

"I see." Nicholas turned his face up towards the sun again, though he no longer seemed to be basking in it quite so happily. "I understand."

"Do you?" Dave sounded sour and sceptical, he knew he did.

Nicholas laughed. "You bring me to this beautiful place to read me the Riot Act … ? How am I meant to take you seriously?"

"Mr Goring," Dave began with stiff formality, "I really must insist –"

"All right, all right! The only rule is to listen to you, and do as you tell me. I get it."

"And you agree?"

"Yes! For heaven's sake," the man softly grumbled.

Dave sighed. He liked to be liked, he knew that about himself. It could be the hardest part of this job that he sometimes had to insist on being completely unlikeable.

And perhaps Nicholas could already read all of that in him, because without any further prompting he offered, "I *do* take your point, and I agree, and I promise I'll behave myself out there. It would break my heart to lose a chance at the butterflies, but if you decide my heart is to be broken, then so be it."

"I wouldn't do anything without reason," Dave offered in turn.

"I trust you entirely."

They'd both paused in their wanderings, and now they stared at each other. Dave had pushed, that was certain, but he hadn't meant to go this deep.

Nicholas shrugged lightly. "I realise I am trusting you entirely, with my life and with more besides. That doesn't necessarily come easily for me, but I'll do it with a good grace."

And all Dave could do was nod in acknowledgement, and then turn to get them moving again. They paced slowly on, shoulder to shoulder. Soon he observed, "I've known Englishmen before. None of them talked like you do."

"Ah, well. I'm not just English, am I?"

"No?"

"I'm the youngest son of an earl. And gay. Incorrigible. And a quarter French."

"That would do it," Dave agreed. He left a pause, but then sought to get the conversation back on a firmer footing. "Okay. Thank you for agreeing. Now, the trick to returning home, safe and whole, is to make sure nothing goes wrong. Nothing at all."

The man's eyebrows climbed. "Is that likely? I was assuming you'd plan for every contingency."

"I do, and I have backups, redundant supplies, emergency procedures. We should never be further than a half day's drive from the nearest bit of civilisation. We'll never be more than a two hour helicopter ride away."

"So … ?"

"We can cope if one or two things go wrong. It wouldn't be a problem. But trouble is like a row of dominoes. Things happen; that precipitates more things happening; it quickly becomes a horrible mess, and we're in the midst of it, dead or injured. And there aren't many second chances in the Outback, you know. Not many at all."

"Look, I assure you that –"

"Camping in the Cotswolds or what–have–you, five minutes from the nearest pub, doesn't cut it. Not the same thing at all."

"All right!" said Nicholas, rather sharply. *"I get the point."*

"Did I scare you a bit?" asked Dave.

"Well. Maybe a bit."

"Good. Thank you. And I'm done now. Unless I think you need another dose sometime to make you see sense."

"Consider it seen," Nicholas stiffly replied. After a moment, he said, as if forcing out the words, "Well. I suppose you need to know that I am on medication."

"I do need to know that, yes. Do you have sufficient supplies? What is the condition? We should probably consult a doctor before we leave."

"That won't be necessary, I assure you. There won't be any problems. It's not that kind of condition."

And he so obviously didn't want to talk about it – and Dave had already pushed so very hard – that Dave took pity on the man. "All right," he said gently. "That's all right." They still had days to go before they left, after all.

When it became clear that Dave wouldn't insist, Nicholas nodded slightly in gratitude. And they finished their walk in silence.

Denise called that evening, and as usual cut right to the chase. "How's your earl?"

"Not an earl."

"Well, your baby earl, then … Which makes him an earling!" she declared with a laugh. "How's your earling?"

Dave frowned for a moment over the day's jumbled impressions, and then ventured, "Unexpected."

"Ah," Denise wisely responded, as if this actually meant something to her. "Are you getting along all right?"

"Yes, it's almost as if … Well, you know how once you've known someone for a while you get past the difficulties, and it's as if you've known them forever already?"

"You get comfortable. Especially when you're on a long trip."

"Yes, and it's just the two of you, and –" He sighed, though it was more in puzzlement than sadness or frustration. "Well, it's kind of like we're there already. Like we just skipped ahead."

"Well, that's good, isn't it? I mean, so you don't drive each other crazy these next three months … ?"

"Yeah. Yeah, um …" He tried to think it through, this sense of unease that accompanied the ease. "Unless the difficulties just come later. I guess."

"You'll be right, mate," she said stoutly.

"Will I?"

"You've been doing this for ages, yeah?"

"Yeah. Six years with Dad; nine on my own."

"Well, you've never yet hit a client over the head with a shovel and buried them under a red gum, have you … ?"

"Actually, no. No, I haven't."

"See? You'll be fine."

two

Five days later Dave drove out of Brisbane in his Land Cruiser, with every space in the back and on the roof rack efficiently crammed with supplies, and Nicholas beside him in the passenger seat. The Englishman sat there quiet and still with his hands resting placid on his long thighs, yet he seemed to *tingle* with anticipation; it was infectious, the very air seemed to sparkle with it. Dave grinned to himself. Despite having done this for most of his life, he was as susceptible to the excitement of a new trip as anyone could be.

And, after all, it wasn't just the trip – it was the new Cruiser that had Dave himself tingling. She was a beauty. He'd just upgraded to the 2011 model in Magnetic Gray with a roo bar, side rails, snorkel, long–range fuel tank, and the rest. This was her first real trip, and to be honest he'd been a little disappointed to know he wouldn't have her to himself for this first stage of the journey. Nicholas remained quiet, though, which allowed Dave the chance to revel in all the joys of his Cruiser. She was solid, of course, but also sleek and smooth, and she handled with just the right responsiveness – easy but not skittish. They were only on regular roads for now, but Dave thrilled to how she held to the planes and curves.

He and Nicholas didn't talk. Not that there was much outside to distract or interest. The Warrego Highway had soon taken them out of the suburbs, and then through apparently endless farmland and towns. Dave had to assume the landscape wasn't very exciting for his English companion, but Nicholas paid careful attention, apparently genuine in his wish to get a feel for the countryside and how it slowly oh–so–slowly changed as they left the coast behind.

They didn't talk. They'd spent that entire first day together talking, then they hadn't seen each other since. Dave had been busy making the last preparations for the trip, and closing up his house. Nicholas, meanwhile, had apparently been happily occupied with the insect collections at the university, the museum, the Department of Primary Industries, and God only knew where else. In fact, they'd been going to meet for dinner on the Tuesday evening, but Nicholas had been so engrossed in his studies that he'd called to cancel at the last minute, having let the afternoon slip by unnoticed. He'd been keen to meet the following day, but Dave hadn't wanted to cancel his plans to spend a last few hours with Denise, Vittorio and little Zoe – especially as it had been made clear that the invitation was issued on behalf of all three of them. Dave might have worried about not getting to know his client well enough under other circumstances, but it seemed to him that they'd connected on that first day; he was blithely confident that any problems between them would be small, and that they could handle them as they came.

After about an hour and a half, the road started winding through what seemed to be real bush. Nicholas smiled happily, and sank a little in his seat as if luxuriating in it. Dave had to disillusion him.

"Make the most of it," he advised. "There's a scrap of bush as we head through the hills, and then we're into Toowoomba."

"The city."

"Yeah. D'you wanna stop for a cuppa tea, or something?"

Nicholas dragged his gaze away from the countryside for a moment. "I'd never say no to tea, but wouldn't you rather keep going? We're not even a quarter of the way there yet, are we?"

"No, but we're not in any hurry. We might as well make the most of it. Like I said before, I don't think we should try doing it all in one day."

"But you would if you were on your own. Wouldn't you?"

"That's different."

"A cup of tea, then," Nicholas concluded. "If you don't mind stopping."

And they were into suburbia again. Dave drove along sedately, barely a kilometre or two – well, maybe five – over the speed limit. "You're the client," he observed mildly. "You can always say if you want a cuppa."

Nicholas smiled at him, softly – and then he changed the subject. "You were right, we would have been halfway to Wales by now."

"We'd have been *in* Wales."

Nicholas laughed, but couldn't help quibbling. "Driving in Britain is qualitatively different, not just quantitatively."

"Spoken like a true scientist."

"It takes a lot longer to get around. It's much more built–up and crowded, so there's more effort involved. There are far fewer empty stretches of road."

"You've got the motorways."

"That's different. And they create their own problems."

Dave shrugged, and found somewhere to park.

A polite request in his English accent and a winsome smile earned Nicholas a pot of tea delivered with a wink – in response to which Nicholas beamed up at their waitress happily. Suzie stood there with a bit of sass in her posture as she considered the man in turn. "Ah, Davey, you can bring this one back any time you like."

"Developing a thing for Poms, are you?" Dave asked with mock sourness.

"With that smile, who cares what flavour he is?"

"That smile?" Dave echoed blankly, having to think for a moment to work out what was wrong with the sentence. Then he got it. "Those smiles," he corrected her. "The man has a whole repertoire."

"Does he indeed … ?" She sounded intrigued.

But Nicholas's attention had been caught by Dave. As he gazed across the rickety old cafe table, his smile turned wistful – though when he spoke, he addressed Suzie. "I would have thought you'd be encouraging David to return for his sake, not for mine."

"Ah," she grieved, taking a metaphorical step back, and snapping her chewing gum. "That's how it is, is it? Well, mate, Davey here is no use to either of us, I'm afraid. He's strictly a one–woman man."

Dave tried not to splutter in protest. "We broke up *ages* ago! A year or more!"

"What's that got to do with anything?"

"She's –" Dave was having second thoughts, but said it anyway, glancing at Nicholas with a plea for rescue. "Denny's married with a kid already! She's *long* gone."

"Uh huh. Whatever you say."

"I'm gonna be, like, the kid's *godparent*."

Suzie looked at him flatly. "I rest my case." And she belatedly put Dave's mug of coffee down, before turning her back and sauntering off.

Dave's mute plea kept Nicholas quiet. Well, he was obviously gay enough to be curious, but at least he was bloke enough to know that some things just couldn't be discussed. "Um," said Dave, scrambling for a different topic of conversation. Just in case. "Um … Oh. Did you learn anything new about your butterflies? I mean, from all those collections?"

Nicholas's gaze turned intent and his smile fond for a long slow moment.

Then he gently chided, "I would have told you, if there was anything that would change our plans."

"I know," Dave responded easily. "Not why I asked."

The smile grew as another moment lengthened. It felt as if Nicholas was happy in their mutual sense of trust. Eventually, Nicholas said, "No. No, if I find them, then there's a chance it will be a new species discovered. There's been very few sightings of the Lycaenidae reported in that area. At least, not of the sort of thing I'm expecting."

"The what?"

"The Family Lycaenidae: the blues. And when I say that area, I mean that entire south–west corner of the state. Though I guess … Well, I am extrapolating rather a lot from very little data. It could all come to nothing, of course."

"Huh." Dave hadn't quite realised the full significance of this quest of discovery. "An entirely new butterfly … You'll be able to give your name to it, then?"

Nicholas was smiling with slow contentment again. "Yes, I will."

"In Latin, like Whatever Goringi. Or Blah–de–blah Nicholasi. Nicholai … ?"

The smile became a laugh. "Something like that."

"Cool."

"And I'll write it up for *The Australian Journal of Entomology*, and I'll say I couldn't have done any of it without Mr David Taylor of Brisbane."

"Fame at last!" Dave laughed. "Thanks, mate."

"Might be good for business."

"Butterfly hunting. Dunno how much call there is for it, to be honest. Most people who brave the Outback are wanting to go crocodile wrestling instead."

"Ah, but if you want to attract the more charmingly eccentric clients …"

Dave couldn't help but grin; Nicholas's wicked brand of happiness was definitely catching. "Well, it's working for me so far," Dave finally agreed.

The Warrego Highway took them north–west from Toowoomba. The countryside around them was still mostly cultivated, but the number of lone houses and small towns slowly decreased. As their journey continued

Nicholas eventually relaxed, realising that he wouldn't miss anything new if he let his attention wander for a moment or two. They still didn't talk much, however.

They stopped for lunch in Chinchilla, and then drove on. A while later the highway turned towards the west; they were getting close to the town of Miles.

"I thought we'd stop there overnight," Dave said into the silence. "Stay at the hotel. Not that there's anything much to do in Miles, but we can drive out into the bush, if you like. Get a better feel for it than we can driving past. And there might be precious few trees where we end up. Might as well enjoy them while we can."

"We can stop?" Nicholas asked. "Do you mind?"

"Course not. I mean, of course I don't mind," Dave clarified. "Just say, whenever."

"Oh, but it's *your* rules," was the teasing response. "What you say goes."

Dave chuckled. "We're not quite at the life–and–death part of the trip yet. But thank you," he found himself adding, "for taking me seriously."

"My pleasure," the man replied with light simplicity.

And Dave metaphorically kicked himself for saying far too much.

Dave had booked them into the hotel rather than the motel, as the narrow rooms with painted eucalypt–green wood–panelled walls felt more genuinely Australian to him. The rooms were each sparsely but elegantly furnished with a single iron bed, a wardrobe, a dressing table and a chair; simple white curtains hung by the tall sash windows. It wasn't the Hilton, but Dave thought Nicholas would appreciate this more than the kind of motel room to be found on road trips anywhere.

They checked in and headed upstairs with their overnight bags. Nicholas chuckled when he discovered that they'd been given adjoining rooms – and then he cast a wink over his shoulder at Dave as he slid past his door and into his room.

Barely a minute later, there was a knock at Dave's door. "End of the corridor on your left!" Dave called out.

"What? Oh!" Another chuckle. "No, I just wanted to say it'd be great to head out again. Whenever you're ready."

"Oh." Dave went to open the door, and considered the man. "You're keen."

"I am. But if you need some time out –"

Dave stretched out an arm to grab the keys from the table. "Let's go, then."

They headed off north past the old cemetery and up Pelham Road for a way, until Dave turned off down a track that took them into the living quiet amidst a scatter of gum trees. Not that it was wilderness or anything, but neither was it like anything else they'd experienced that day – or would again, probably, for several days to come. Nicholas was all hushed expectancy, staring around them as Dave drove along at a fair pace.

Once he felt they'd left civilisation as far behind as they could for now, Dave said, "What d'you want to see? What are you looking for?"

"Anything." Nicholas turned to him, his dark blue eyes alight with eagerness. "Honestly. Anything. There's still so much to discover here!"

"Well, it's your first trip …"

"No, I mean – Australia's so *vast*. And there's so few people really studying it. You'd be astonished – Well, maybe you wouldn't be. But the discoveries people make! And the things that have been found and then lost again … And the place is so *old* –" Nicholas stopped with a laugh. "What am I telling you all this for? You'd know it better than me."

"I dunno, not really," Dave admitted. "I mean, I know *bits* of it. Sounds like you've got a bigger perspective. And I'm not – I never went to college or anything. I liked geology in high school though."

"That's all right – you've been living it. Not just reading about it, like me."

"So we both know different things," Dave tried. "Or we're coming at it from different angles."

"We're going to have *so much* to talk about," Nicholas concluded rather happily.

Dave glanced away. "Where d'you want me to stop?"

"Here," said Nicholas, without even looking.

And Dave immediately pulled over, even though it was a completely random place. He parked carefully, just off the track, despite them not having seen any other traffic since they'd left Miles. Nicholas grinned at him for a moment, before slowly turning away, unfastening his seat belt and letting it slide home. Then he opened the passenger door and carefully stepped out.

Dave got out, too, and headed around the back of the Cruiser to retrieve a box. He may or may not have patted the Cruiser's rear in grateful admiration, he wouldn't like to say. Then he continued on round to find that Nicholas had barely taken a step. He'd barely even moved, but seemed to be looking here and there, his eyes darting, as if torn over which direction to take.

"Here," said Dave – and Nicholas turned a grateful gaze upon him, as if glad to have the matter decided for him, at least for now. "Here, I got you this."

Nicholas was as delighted as a kid at Christmas. He reached to carefully take the box in both hands, and beamed happily at Dave. It was perfectly obvious what it was from the branding on the box, never mind that Dave had already announced he'd buy this for him. Nevertheless, Dave was blown away by the power of Nicholas's smile. He watched as, with a kind of awe, Nicholas unfolded the box, unwrapped the tissue paper, took out the Akubra – and marvelled at it for long moments before slipping it on. It fit neatly, and looked just as Dave had imagined.

Nicholas's smile grew so overwhelming that Dave scrambled for refuge in words. He had to clear his throat before he could voice anything meaningful, mind. "It's the classic style. You know? The Cattleman."

"It's like yours," Nicholas observed.

Dave had put on his own old Cattleman as soon as he'd gotten out of the Cruiser. It was part of him, and had been for more years than he could remember. His father had bought it for him … well, it must have been for his eighteenth.

"It's perfect!" Nicholas was continuing. "How did you know –"

"I emailed your butler, and asked him how big your head was. He said *very*."

Nicholas went pink round the cheekbones. "He did not."

"Nah. He sent me your measurements. Well, you know. For hats, anyway."

"And the colour?"

It was the Bluegrass Green. Dave had been going to get the Sand, like his own, because that was also classic. But then he'd thought about Nicholas's black hair and dark blue eyes. The blue jeans he'd worn on that first day, with the sage green t–shirt, and the black sweater. Nicholas was wearing blue, black and green again today. And Dave had thought about how the darker hat colours – the Black, the Graphite Gray, the Western Navy – would absorb the heat. He'd thought again about the unsettlingly oceanic depths of Nicholas's eyes. And he'd gone for the Bluegrass Green.

"You asked him about the colour, too?" Nicholas persisted.

"What?"

"You asked Simon about the colour … ?"

"Oh." Dave could feel his cheeks heating. "No, I just guessed."

"It's *perfect*." Nicholas had it in his hands again, turning it about, and admiring it. When he went to put it back on again, he grinned at Dave – and made the usual rookie mistake. He pinched the crown at the front between his thumb and second finger, and lifted it one–handed.

"Not like that!" Dave cried, instinctively reaching for Nicholas's narrow wrist to stop him. God, now they were both blushing. Dave took his hand away.

Luckily, Nicholas didn't take offence at any of that. "What did I do wrong?" he asked, apparently keen to know the answer.

"I know that's how they hold it in the movies. And it looks good, doesn't it? I mean, it's like you should be able to hold the crown like that. But you'll put pressure on the creases here, and that's where it'll end up cracking. Maybe not for years, but you don't wanna –"

"No, I don't," Nicholas agreed.

"Um, so, you know, it should last you a long long while …" He trailed off uncertainly.

"So, how should I hold it?"

Dave looked, and snorted as he saw the Akubra's brim now warily balanced on the very tips of Nicholas's long fingers. "Not like that, either! Here, you can grasp it as strong as you like with both hands, at the front and back." He demonstrated with his own hat, taking it off, and then putting it back on again. "Fit the front low on your forehead, then push it down at the back until it's in place … That's it," he added approvingly, surveying the results.

Nicholas was still smiling, gratefully. Even with a wry kind of sweetness. "Thank you," he said, in tones that matched his smile.

"You're welcome," Dave responded, feeling completely at a loss now.

And it seemed that even Nicholas was, too, for he finally turned away, and slowly wandered off, apparently scanning the undergrowth in search of something. Hiding his face, when he could, behind the lowered hat brim.

Dave followed him, watching him, occasionally glimpsing those pretty pink lips, slightly parted now in concentration. How strange it was, Dave pondered, that he'd become so very fixed upon Nicholas's marvellous smiles. How very wrong it was to be thinking so much about another bloke's mouth …

The quiet of the bush was calming. A delicious full silence was augmented by the occasional bell–like chirp of a bird, the bustle of a four–footed creature carrying on with life unconcerned by these two human intruders. Dave sighed contentedly. Flora and fauna weren't his strong suit, beyond the necessary survival knowledge of what he could eat in an emergency and what he couldn't, but he really did love it out here, in the bush, in the Outback. He loved that, mostly, the flora and fauna were willing to coexist with him, if he only paid them their due respect.

Dry bark crunched under Nicholas's footfall, and Dave's attention was back on him again. The Englishman was moving slowly, peering about at the lower shrubs, at the ground, at the sparse grasses – ducking and frowning now and then, weaving to and fro, until – "There! My first Australian butterfly."

"What?"

"Well, my first one in the wild, as it were."

Dave eased closer, astonished. "You're making discoveries already?"

"No. Oh, no … This is just a Cabbage White or one of the Pearl Whites, I should think. I'll have to check the field guide."

"What is?" Dave asked dumbly, looking about for beautiful white wings. "Where?"

"Here." Nicholas crouched, and indicated a grub–like casing. "It's in the pupa stage. One day, not too far distant, it will break apart, and the most glorious butterfly will emerge."

"Oh. Oh, of course." Dave felt like an idiot. He'd done some research, but then he'd also felt that the butterflies were Nicholas's area, and the organisation and safety of their travel were Dave's. Apparently his reading – or, more to the point, his browsing – had gone in one eye and out the other …

Nicholas had straightened up to consider Dave a bit kindly, as if he were to be pitied. "You know nothing about butterflies, do you?"

"They're pretty, I know that much."

"Yes, they are."

"I like the colours," Dave babbled, probably not redeeming himself. "When I was browsing Google images, I liked the blue ones best."

Nicholas was nodding earnestly. "Ours – *our* butterflies – are going to be *gorgeous*. Like bits of the sky come alive." He took a step closer to Dave, his hands in the air between them as if trying to shape adequate words. "But you're only thinking about their last stage of life. They *transform*."

"They do," Dave agreed, looking at the pupa, which might as well be an old bit of stick. "Is that – is that why you're so interested? In butterflies, I mean. Because of how they change so much?"

"Sorry … What?"

"I was just wondering," Dave blundered on: "*Why* butterflies?"

But Nicholas had taken a step back, and his long face sobered. It was as if the sun had gone in.

All right. Time to change tack. "D'you want to walk about a bit more?" Dave asked. "Seeing as we're out here."

A brief nod.

"We'll get the field guide, eh? Is it in the Cruiser?"

"Yes," was the quiet reply.

Dave hardly spoke after that, not wanting to spoil things any further. They went back and fetched Nicholas's satchel which contained his guide, his camera, a notebook and pens. And then Dave followed around as Nicholas ducked and weaved, searching around at random, and he kept track of where they'd left the Cruiser. It didn't take too long – not even half an hour, really – before the peace settled over them again.

three

They were into the acacia scrub the next day, as they headed west for Charleville. The gum trees grew sparser, and the acacia shrubs took over with tussocks of dry grass dotted about, and plenty of bare red–brown dirt between. The land was quickly flattening out. A lot of people hated this semi–arid countryside, and Dave would agree that none of the individual elements were particularly attractive. There was a spartan kind of elemental beauty about the overall effect, though. And he knew that it harboured all kinds of life, some secretive and some not. It was in a landscape such as this, he thought, that Nicholas would find his butterflies.

Nicholas was sitting in the passenger seat looking around with that strangely childlike eagerness of his. It was really quite endearing, but Dave couldn't help teasing. "Don't soak it *all* in at once. Take your time. We'll be seeing a lot of this."

"Yes?"

"We might see nothing *but* acacia scrub, depending on how far afield we go. It'll thin out more as we head west, and it'll be mostly low–level. You're gonna get bored with it pretty quickly."

"Not yet, though," Nicholas said with a grin. "Um … Can we stop?"

"Sure." Dave glanced in the rear–view mirror, just in case, but there was nothing between them and the horizon in either direction. He pulled the Cruiser over, taking it safely off the road. Kept his gaze tactfully averted. "Loo roll in the glove box, if you need it."

"Oh! No. Thank you, but no."

"Well, then. Let's go see how many grubs you can find."

Nicholas grinned, put on his Akubra, grabbed his satchel, and clambered out of the Cruiser. "It's all useful," he explained with endearing earnestness as Dave trailed around after him. "It's like I said: there's so few people working on this. Any reliable observation is welcome."

"That's great." Dave obligingly held items as necessary, kept an eye out for anything Nicholas might find interesting just in case he didn't notice it himself, and made engaged or impressed noises occasionally as Nicholas nattered away.

At some point after Dave's attention had wandered, Nicholas abruptly sat down in the dirt, and Dave stepped towards him anxiously thinking, *Could this guy be any gawkier?* and, *How the hell am I gonna keep him safe?*

But of course Nicholas was fine. He sat there offering a dazed smile to Dave, and said, "I just looked up."

"Oh yes. The sky."

"It's rather larger than the one we have at home."

Dave put his head back and looked up. There wasn't a cloud to interrupt the enormous arc of pure blue, which if you didn't – scarily – let into your soul, would indeed make anyone feel insignificant. Dave huffed a breath. "You matter to me. If not to the sky."

"It's not that so much. I got dizzy there. Just for a moment."

"Like you'd fall up into it?"

"Yes. And float away."

"I'll keep you grounded. It's all right."

Nicholas looked down at his hands for a moment, as the long pale fingers meshed together. "Is that another reason for the hats? To keep the sky out?"

"No! No, you'll get used to it." Dave chuckled. "Wait until you see it at night." Out here, with few lights around, the stars were beyond awesome. Dave had never yet gotten tired of it.

"Spectacular?"

"You got it. Not tonight while we're in Charleville. Wait till we're camping out."

Nicholas grinned, and lifted a hand, which Dave grasped. "I will," Nicholas murmured as he unfolded from the ground, some of his weight a not unwanted test of Dave's strength, and the rest borne up by those long thighs. Nicholas didn't move away once he was standing again. Not immediately. He stayed there for a moment, right up into Dave's space, and whispered in Dave's ear, "I'll wait for you to show me."

Dave tilted his head in closer, as if about to confide in the other man – but what he said was, "You promised you wouldn't flirt."

"Not *my* fault you're so gorgeous, not to mention promising me spectacular nights."

"Huh." Dave stepped away. So gorgeous, yes, he reflected sourly, when the only person he'd ever wanted to hold such an opinion had proved it untrue just over a year ago. And that was that. It hardly mattered if some eccentric English earling had taken it into his head to feel attracted. Dave muttered a few choice swear words under his breath, and kicked disconsolately at the nearest shrub – which sat there, sturdy and unmoved.

"David …" Nicholas sounded infinitely compassionate, all sorrow and grace.

"Leave it be," Dave insisted. Then he said, rather more reasonably, "Take your time. There's no hurry. I'll wait with the Cruiser."

"Of course." And Nicholas crouched to examine something at ground level, his Bluegrass Green Akubra tilting to hide his face.

Dave made as cool an exit as he could.

When Nicholas finally returned to the Cruiser, Dave was deep into *The Nutmeg of Consolation* – and he felt all the better for it. He lifted his head once Nicholas had clambered back into the passenger seat, to find the man smiling at him fondly.

"You're a reader," Nicholas commented. "That actually explains a great deal."

"Not really." Dave shrugged.

"You like the Aubrey–Maturin novels, though? That's wonderful! And what else?"

"There's twenty of them," Dave explained. "Twenty–one if you count the last, but it was only half done when he died. When I finish, I just go back to the start again."

Nicholas laughed, though he sounded more delighted than cruel.

"I've read *The Last of the Mohicans*. And *Moby Dick*. But mostly just these. Denise is the serious reader. She loves George Eliot – who's a woman. And Tchaikovsky."

Nicholas took a breath, and glanced at him askance, before deliberately not saying anything.

"All right, so I've got the name wrong again, don't I?"

"Um … Dostoyevsky?" Nicholas hazarded.

"That's the bloke," Dave equably agreed. He didn't pretend to be educated, after all, but he did love these novels. "I think I'll be reading these all my life."

"I can't think of anything better," said Nicholas.

They reached Charleville late that afternoon, checked into the hotel, and then met half an hour later in the lobby. Despite the fact that they had adjoining rooms again, Dave had been very firm on the location for their rendezvous, and he went down early, while he could still hear Nicholas moving around next door, apparently taking his time unpacking and freshening up.

Once Nicholas joined him, they headed off down the street to the pub that was Charlie's regular. The westering sun bathed them in gold as they walked along side by side.

"Now," said Dave, breaking the silence in his best *this is me setting the rules* voice. "We need to be tactful here. We're not gonna blunder in where we're not wanted, all right?"

"Yes, David," Nicholas replied with a fair crack at a *this is me being the meek and obedient client* voice. The trouble being that it was always undermined – *always*, Dave had learned this already – by a happy little smirk loitering around the man's shapely pink lips.

"Charlie's a mate; we go back for years. We'll say g'day and I'll introduce you, just as soon as it feels right. I mean, just like with anyone. He might already be hanging out with his friends, or something. I mean, his own people. In which case, we don't interrupt unless it's clear we're welcome."

Nicholas nodded, seriously. Apparently now hanging upon every word.

"It's not that Charlie's not completely comfortable in both cultures. But if he's hanging with his Aboriginal friends, then we don't expect him to switch over to our register right away."

"No, of course."

"And once we're talking, then you need to take your cue from me, all right? When you start asking about Dreamtime stuff, then you go easy, and you have a care about whose toes you might be stepping on. If something's secret, then it's secret, and we're not pushing to know who or what or why."

"I understand, David."

"Do you? And can you stick to it? Cos all you can do is explain yourself and ask, right? You can't have any expectations about getting any answers. And even if you sense he's holding back, you've got to let it be his decision."

"Well, you know," Nicholas responded with at last a spark of ire, "I'm not a complete boor."

"I *do* know that," Dave said. "I'm just trying to say – that even more tact is called for than usual."

Nicholas huffed out a breath. "One day I'm going to look back at this and laugh. An Australian teaching an Englishman about tact!"

They'd reached the pub, so Dave led the way through the door, too caught up in the argument to pay any real attention beyond registering that the place was as crowded as usual. He turned back to Nicholas, and let the noisy buzz of the pub's patrons give him an excuse to raise his voice. "Oh yeah, cos you Poms have learned so much from hundreds of years of good relations with the Aboriginals, haven't you?"

Nicholas had been about to take his Akubra off, in an instinctive politeness, but Dave shook his head in annoyance and, after a glance around, Nicholas must have realised that no man took his hat off in such a place. He pushed it back on, and stood tall. "Don't try to pretend, *mate*," Nicholas crisply replied, "that you're not on the white side of the equation. All this pussyfooting around makes you look like part of the problem, not the solution."

"Respect isn't pussyfooting!"

"I'll respect him enough to just tell him straight out what I need, and then I'll leave it to him to decide what he tells me."

"That's what I was asking you to do!" Dave cried in frustration.

"You were not; you were telling me. And I didn't need to be told."

Dave found himself completely undermined by an unexpected fondness as he contemplated the folded arms, affronted shoulders, and loftily lifted nose of his client. He let out a laugh under his breath. "Nicholas," he started in mollifying tones –

"Nicholas … ? Nicholas Goring!"

It was Charlie, of course. Nicholas had already turned towards the enquiring voice, and now he burst into a happy grin. "Charles!" The two men shook hands enthusiastically, while Dave looked on in bewilderment. "How marvellous!" Nicholas was saying. "I didn't dare hope it was you David was bringing me to meet."

"Who else would it be?" Once Charlie was finally done with Nicholas, he turned to greet Dave, and they shook hands, too.

"Hello, Charlie," Dave said, not too grudgingly. He wasn't going to ask, though. The world was a small place, after all. He already knew that.

"We follow each other on Twitter," Nicholas explained, and he was actually sounding friendly, and rather apologetic.

"Come on," Charlie said, leading the way. "Let's get a table, and some beer."

"I'm sorry, David. I should have said."

"No, I shouldn't have assumed."

"Nicholas here is *all right*," Charlie assured Dave as they all sat. In fact, Charlie dragged Nicholas down to sit very close beside him, Dave noted to his own annoyance and chagrin. "Nicholas has Butterfly Dreaming, you know?"

Nicholas laughed happily. "Oh, now you're just flattering me. David's not going to believe that any more than I do."

"Anyway, you're Australian now, Nicholas. You've got the hat."

The man's cheekbones went a happy pink. "David gave it to me."

"Did he now … ?" Charlie turned a pondering gaze on Dave.

"I'm sure he does the same for all his clients."

"Not that I ever heard of," Charlie replied.

"Oh shut up," Dave grumbled.

"In *fact*," Charlie continued as if he hadn't even heard, "I'd say you were in like Flynn there, Nicholas …"

The man's bashfully pleased pinkness bloomed further.

Before Charlie added with regret, "If only Dave weren't a one-woman man."

"Oh God!" Dave cried. "You all think you know what you're talking about, but you don't. You just don't."

"We don't?" Charlie asked.

"No. That's just –" He made it a rule not to swear around clients, even if they expected him to. "Nonsense. That's just nonsense."

Charlie put his head back and considered Dave for a long long moment … before nudging Nicholas with an elbow. "In like Flynn, mate."

Nicholas guffawed quite happily.

"Fuck's sake," muttered Dave. And he went to get a round of beer.

Despite the pub's incessant cheerful noise, Dave was close enough to hear that Charlie and Nicholas were soon nattering away about Dreamtime sites and blue clouds and stone-curlews. Dave shook his head in self-mocking disbelief. So much for tact! He was sure that Charlie would fill him in if they reached any practical conclusions, so he was happy enough to leave them to it.

While waiting to order, Dave thumbed through to a browser on his phone. He'd joined Twitter a couple of years ago, because Denise had gotten into it, but he'd hardly even looked at it since they'd broken up. He was already connected to Charlie, of course. And as soon as he started scrolling through Charlie's list of followers, he found Nicholas. His profile image was, unsurprisingly, a photo of a beautiful blue butterfly. Dave thumbed the Follow button, and then started browsing the man's tweets. Nothing particularly significant, beyond an excitement over the prospect of this trip. Otherwise it seemed to be chat with a wide variety of friends, interspersed with vaguely philosophical questions relating to a butterfly's life and transformation. *Does the butterfly remember its former larval self?* Dave read. Another one earlier in the timeline: *What does a pupa dream of while becoming fabulous?*

Nicholas my man, Charlie had replied to that one, *you tell me. What did YOU dream of?*

No, I'm still the caterpillar. I'm not fabulous yet.

Are you so sure about that, my friend?

Charles, I'm hardly even dreaming yet …

Dave looked up, and found Nicholas's deep dark blue gaze upon him, and for a moment the world around them went still and quiet. They stared at each other, and Dave knew. He knew, somehow, that something within Nicholas had changed since that exchange of tweets. Something that wouldn't – that couldn't change back. He wondered if …

But then Charlie nudged Nicholas and indicated a location on the map they had spread before them, and Rosie behind the bar asked, "You right, Dave?" and the moment was gone.

Dave frowned, pretending to be considering which beers they had on tap. But it was a no–brainer, and Rosie knew it. "Three Cascades, thanks, mate."

When he got back to the table, Nicholas and Charlie still had their heads bent close together over the map. Charlie sat back, and accepted the beer with a grateful nod. The glass was already beading with condensation. Nicholas accepted his, too, with a happy smile – and then he turned to consider Charlie for a long moment. Took in Charlie's thoughtfulness, and then tactfully lowered his gaze. Waiting, with no expectation. Sipping at his beer.

If Nicholas had looked up at Dave in those moments, Dave suspected that he would have found a very fond expression looking back at him. Perhaps it was as well that he didn't.

Half of Dave's Cascade slid coolly down a welcoming throat.

Eventually Charlie sat up, and said to Nicholas, "Show me again."

"Here," murmured Nicholas, one of his long pale fingers marking a rough circle towards the south–west corner of Queensland. "This sort of area."

Charlie nodded, and glanced at each of them in turn, taking their measure. Then he pressed a finger–pad to a place within the lower half of the circle. "Here. Stay north of here, I reckon. That's just a guess," he added, "from an old fella who hasn't been out that way in a *long* time."

"No, that's great," Dave said, knowing that Charlie had just shared a secret with them, even if only implicitly. "Thank you."

"Thank you," Nicholas echoed, with exactly the right quiet restraint. "I really appreciate it, Charles."

Charlie sat back again, relaxed, and downed half his beer. "We've got to find you your butterflies," he said to Nicholas. "I think … we'll all learn something from them."

"I'll do my best."

"Don't wanna have come all this way for nothing," Charlie continued, his expansive gesture somehow taking in Dave as well as the butterflies.

Nicholas went pink round the cheekbones, and laughed. It was a delightful sound. Which Dave might even have appreciated if he hadn't been so set on muttering complaints under his breath.

And Dave wasn't even halfway done grumbling yet, when Nicholas obligingly offered, "I'll get the next, uh – shout."

Charlie crowed with laughter. "You're even talking Strine now, mate!"

Nicholas grinned, but dipped his head towards Dave to surreptitiously ask, "What exactly do I order?"

"Three Cascades," Dave supplied. "And say thanks, not please."

An uncomplicated pleasure broadened the grin. "Three Cascades, thanks," Nicholas practised.

Dave nodded encouragement, and ignored Charlie's wondering look until Nicholas was safely at the bar, attention fixed on sorting through the colourful Australian dollar notes in his wallet. And then Dave said, "What?"

despite knowing exactly.

"You can't even stay angry at him," Charlie observed.

"Oh God, will you *please* give it a rest."

"Mate, you didn't even set him up for a fall just then."

"Course not. He's a client."

"Ah, come on. Classic chance for a bit of fun, and I know you've done it before. Rosie would have played along, too, and you know it."

"Look," said Dave, determined to take this chance at least. He propped his elbows on the table and leaned in closer to talk in confidence. "How well do you know him? Nicholas, I mean."

"Yeah, who else would you be obsessing over?"

"How well?" Dave insisted.

"Hhhmmm …" Charlie responded in a quibbling manner.

"It's just that his butler or whatever told me to treat him kindly, but wouldn't explain what he meant."

"Maybe he didn't mean anything."

"No, he did."

"Then maybe he just meant that Nicholas is a nice guy. Worth looking after."

It wasn't enough. Dave shook his head.

"And coming out here all alone," Charlie persisted. "He just wanted to make sure that Nicholas could count on you."

"There has to be something more specific. There has to be."

"What are you worried about? He looks fine! Happy as. Nice bit of a glow to him."

Dave nodded reluctantly. "He *has* got more colour to him lately. I reckon it's being out in the sun, despite the hat."

"See? He's fine."

"Dunno …"

"Davey," said Charlie.

"Yeah?"

"You worry too much, mate. You'll be fine. *Both* of you – will be fine."

Well, and Dave could only hope it was true.

Late that night Dave lay awake listening to the quiet rustling of rhythmic movement against bedclothes audible from the next room, and Nicholas's gentle panting breaths. Dave wondered if Nicholas was thinking about him. It already felt inevitable that that was the case. On the other hand, if Dave was going to leap to such conclusions, he should probably just get over himself instead. He wasn't the centre of anyone's universe. Not anymore.

Nicholas finished soon enough with a soft groan, and then quiet fell through the hotel, through the town, through the countryside surrounding them. The hush was vibrant, though. Energised with longing. Somehow Dave got the impression that Nicholas was lying there still awake. Not quite satisfied.

Dave sighed, and turned away. Settled himself for sleep with his back towards the wall he shared with Nicholas. As if even that mattered. He closed his eyes, and with another lonely sigh slipped away into the dark.

four

Dave was at the Cruiser early the next morning with his checklist, making sure they had all they needed. He couldn't think of anything he'd missed, anything they'd need to visit the Charleville shops for – and that in itself worried him. It would almost be a relief to think of something he'd forgotten. Dave sighed, and slid the checklist away with his other paperwork.

Which was when Nicholas appeared from the hotel in a bit of a flurry, with his black shirt buttoned up yet misaligned. He was barefoot, but already had on his Akubra. "Am I running late? I haven't packed yet. Won't take me a minute, though. Good idea of yours, to have a separate overnight bag," Nicholas added, before squinting up at the sky. "But I didn't oversleep, did I?"

Dave chuckled. "Nah, I'm just doing a last check through. Think we'll be fine – but this is your last chance for any shopping for a week."

A cloud passed across that long mutable face. "I should think that I can manage without shopping for a week." The gay man was offended.

"I just meant that if you need any essentials …"

But Nicholas was grinning again, with a mischievous little kick to it. "I know."

Dave just rolled his eyes. "*Anyway*," he continued, "we've got to have one of Billy's full cooked breakfasts before we go. Won't need to eat again until we're back in civilisation."

"Cool, okay. And then –" Nicholas's smile was quieter now, but pure and true – and Dave really had to quit obsessing over the man's smiles for God's sake! "And then we'll be off for real."

"Yup. Off like a bucket of prawns in the hot sun."

"What?"

"Never mind. Yeah, we'll be out into the beyond." Dave wasn't immune to the excitement of it, even after all these years. But he touched a hand to Nicholas's suitcase where one side of it appeared amidst all their belongings and gear and necessaries – and he frowned. "Um … Got your medication all right?"

"Yes, darling," Nicholas replied in a long-suffering spouse voice.

"Good. Yeah. Bit anal about this sort of thing."

"It's life and death!" Nicholas protested. "Of course you take it seriously."

Dave grinned at him. "All right, all right. Now, go back up and get your shoes. I can't have you wandering around the Outback barefoot any more than you can be bareheaded."

"I *did* remember the Akubra," Nicholas commented with mock innocence.

"I am *not* buying you shoes as well," Dave responded with mock severity. "Go on! And then we can have breakfast, just as soon as you're ready."

"David, I am *always* ready …"

Dave just growled – and Nicholas scarpered with a gurgling giggle.

Nicholas didn't even want to stop for a cup of tea late that morning – their last chance for one that they didn't make themselves – so Dave kept driving, and they shared a bottle of water. Within a couple of hours, they were into the search area – which was massive. While they were still around the edges, at least, Dave had negotiated Nicholas down from stopping every mile to stopping every ten kilometres. They'd pull over, and Nicholas would look around, identify anything butterfly–related that he found, take handwritten notes, photograph it. And then they'd drive on. He didn't discover much, and nothing unexpected, though sometimes the identification would take a while of frowning over the guide.

At one point in the early afternoon, they found a flurry of white butterflies amassed over a particular spot that looked just the same as any other to Dave in the relatively featureless scrub. Nicholas lit up like it was Christmas – God only knew what he'd look like when they found his blues. They pulled over, and by the time Nicholas was done recording all the pertinent details, Dave had set up two folding chairs in the shade of the Cruiser, and brought out cold drinks and the makings of sandwiches for lunch. They sat there together watching the drift and hover of tiny scraps of white against the huge curve of bright blue sky. Nicholas was just *wallowing* in the sight.

But Dave was prompted to raise something that had given him pause. "How do we find a *blue* cloud? I mean, I can *see* this. And I get the cloud idea. But how on earth do we spot them against a blue sky?"

Nicholas was too happy to doubt. "If Clemence Hall could see them, we'll be able to, too."

"Maybe we need it to be overcast, so the blue shows up against the white haze."

But Nicholas shook his head. "Not if they only fly in the direct sunshine. Butterflies have to be warm enough to be able to fly, you see. Otherwise, they remain settled."

"That's why they only fly during the day," Dave said with a sense of realisation.

"Yes." Nicholas looked at him, obviously knowing there was more and waiting for it.

Dave shook his head. "A story I heard once. I'll have to remember it properly before I tell you."

"All right," Nicholas agreed contentedly.

They sat there for a while longer.

Eventually Dave cleared his throat. "Is there more to see?"

Nicholas turned to him with an apologetic look. "Can we wait until they settle again? Any observation –"

"– is useful, yes. No worries," Dave added. And he relaxed a little further down into his chair. He might have even nodded off in the mid–afternoon warmth …

When Dave opened his eyes again he found the Cruiser's shadow stretching out further beyond his feet, and Nicholas's warm amused gaze on him – and Nicholas's hand resting lightly on Dave's forearm. As soon as Dave stirred, Nicholas's hand lifted away and resettled against the shirt over his chest. Pressed flat over his breastbone. Dave eyed him with a frown, still only half awake.

"Sorry," Nicholas offered, "I thought you'd want to –"

"Of course," Dave agreed. He reached for the water bottle, and poured a bit of life back into himself. "Of course, yeah." He sat up straighter, and checked his watch. Almost five already. Then he thought to look for the butterflies. And found the air was empty for as far as he could see. "Have they –"

"– settled for the night. Yes."

"So should we." Dave frowned in thought for a moment. "One more ten–

click stage," he suggested, "and then we find somewhere to set up camp."

"Only one … ?"

"It's our first camp. It'll take us a while to get set up. Better make sure we have plenty of daylight to do it in."

Nicholas nodded. "All right, yes. I understand."

"Good." Dave drank some more water, and felt revived enough to continue. "I'll pack this lot up, if you're ready."

"I'm ready," Nicholas said. "I'll help."

"Thank you."

Of course the reality was that on a trip everyone had to pitch in and help one way or another. And with only two of them, there was just as much to do in many ways, and fewer people to do it with. Dave had warned Nicholas, of course, and he knew that Nicholas was more than willing to help, but until they got started Dave had been sceptical about how much the Englishman would be capable of. He was the son of an earl who had servants, for a start. He might have gotten away with never having to do much that he didn't want to. Not to mention that the man was slim to the point of scrawny, with pale almost translucent skin.

In the event, Nicholas was tireless, and seemed possessed of a supple wiry strength Dave hadn't even suspected. Not like delicate fine china at all. He cheerfully did all that he was asked, and more, too, when he saw something that needed doing. Well, he was cheerful right through the task of putting up Nicholas's tent. But his face fell when he realised that they were about to put up a second tent for Dave. His face fell, and then resentment sparked in those deep dark eyes.

"Do you really not trust me?"

"It's not that," Dave said uncomfortably.

"I'm not the kind of guy to insist where I'm not welcome. I *promise* I'm not."

"I know," said Dave. "I know."

"These tents are … well, not enormous. But certainly large enough for two."

"They'll sleep four if necessary. I usually allocate a tent for every two or three people."

Nicholas stared at him hard. "Well, then?"

"Don't you appreciate having your own space?"

The stare flickered a little, and some of the righteousness ebbed away. "I suppose. Yes." Nicholas sighed. "Yes."

"I always have my own tent," Dave explained. "*Always*. It's one of my rules. And no one gets to come in. That's my space, d'you see?"

Nicholas sagged a little further. "Yes, of course. I do see."

"It's nothing to do with you. I mean, no more than any client."

"I understand."

"Good." Dave turned away. It's not as if anything would have happened, anyway, whether they shared a tent or not. Such a thing didn't even factor into his calculations.

"I suppose you have a non–fraternisation rule, too. You'd never sleep with a client, would you?"

"Of course not."

A beat of silence. Another.

"Come on, then," Nicholas said with a friendly kind of briskness. "This tent isn't going to assemble itself."

And Dave turned back to the man with an appreciative laugh.

Dave lit a campfire, of course. Partly for warmth, partly for the focus it provided, partly because it was expected. He set a billy to boil over it for bush tea, but otherwise cooked their meat, potatoes and veg on the gas stove. While waiting for dinner to be ready, he pottered about happily, organising everything just so. And he didn't forget to call Denise on the satphone, to give her their coordinates and reassure her that all was well. Dave might have wandered around the far side of the Cruiser before making the call, but that didn't signify anything. In any case, Denise only had time to jot down the details, as Zoe was crying for attention, though she made a point of telling him to take care. Which warmed his heart, even now. Dave hung up, and went to attend to his own charge.

Dinner was a success. Nicholas ate ravenously and gratefully – and, as he finally set his empty plate aside, declared, "That was delicious!"

"Food always tastes better outdoors."

The man laughed, but insisted, "No, it was really great."

"Thank you." Dave measured out the tea into the billy, and added a couple of gum leaves he'd saved for the purpose, then left it to steep. "Come on," he said, beckoning to Nicholas. "Come away from the fire."

Nicholas cast a somewhat nervous look around them. "Are you sure? Why?" He'd stood up, though, and stepped after Dave. "What's out there?" he asked in hushed tones, as if predators could be avoided by whispering.

"Nothing. Don't worry."

But Nicholas's hand had slid into Dave's, just as easily as if Dave had been holding it out in invitation. Trust the gay English earling to interpret his gesture that way! But when Dave turned to tell him off, he discovered a wide–eyed Nicholas, honestly innocent and genuinely fearful.

"If there's anything out there, it's either asleep or it'll avoid you if you give it the chance. I promise. You'll be fine."

Nicholas's hand squeezed his, as if returning his reassurance. "Then what –"

"Just keep your back to the fire. Let your eyes adjust."

They did that, walking away from the fire, with Dave leading Nicholas, hand in hand. Picking their way through the scrub, keeping an intent gaze on where they were putting their feet.

Finally they were ready. Dave came to a halt, and Nicholas settled beside him, watching him trustingly.

"Now," said Dave, "look up."

And rather than take in the wonders of the night sky himself, Dave watched Nicholas's stunned reaction. He gaped, and swayed back for a moment as if he'd find himself abruptly sitting down again. "Oh my ..." he murmured. Dave had let go of Nicholas in order to put his hand to the man's back, keeping him upright. Nicholas similarly grasped a goodly portion of Dave's shirt in one hand, hanging on. Hanging on. Somehow restraining himself from actually touching Dave, though, for which Dave gave him points.

So many more of the stars were visible out here that it seemed like some kind of miracle. Some completely different universe, perhaps, or more than one, intermingling its beauties with the Earth's familiar skies.

"Oh, David," Nicholas murmured.

"I know."

"You don't even guess at all this. Not even from the country, let alone a city. In England, I mean."

"It's just the lack of other lights out here," Dave explained. "We're so far from anything now. This is always there, above our heads. We just don't see it."

After a moment, Dave realised that Nicholas had lowered his head and was staring at Dave with much the same kind of wonder. "That's very wise."

"Is it?"

"Don't you think …" Nicholas slowly began. "That's such a metaphor. For our lives, I mean. The beauty is there – the awesome beauty – but we just don't see it. Most of the time it's right above our heads, and we walk along oblivious."

Dave shrugged uncomfortably. "I was just talking about the stars. I don't know that there's any life lessons to be had here."

Nicholas considered him for a moment, thoughtful. And then he deliberately let go of Dave, and stood alone. Dave let his hand drop, and was almost sorry for it. Nicholas turned his face up to the stars again, and now Dave did, too.

"I'm sorry," Nicholas eventually murmured. "I was making a philosophical mountain out of what should be simply a lovely experience."

"It's all right," Dave muttered uncomfortably.

"Some of us need a little more faith to cling to, that's all."

Dave made a fairly agreeable yet neutral noise, and left it at that. The stars were so very spectacular … He found himself wondering, though, what Nicholas really needed. And why.

Dave woke early, as he usually did – though if he didn't have any particular plans for the day, he was partial to returning to bed for a further snooze. That morning, however, once he'd seen to the necessaries, Dave discovered that Nicholas was already up – and perhaps had been for some while, even though it was still mostly dark. The eastern horizon was just beginning to lighten. And Nicholas was sitting perched on the roo bar of the Cruiser, with a blanket wrapped around his shoulders.

He cast Dave an apologetic smile as he walked closer. "Good morning. I hope I didn't wake you."

"Morning. No, you didn't. This is kinda my usual time." Dave figured

Nicholas must have been very quiet; Dave usually had a sense for what was happening within his own campsite. "How long have you been up?"

"Oh, an hour or more. I wanted to see the stars again. I wanted to watch the sunrise."

"Of course," said Dave, as if this were the most natural thing on earth. Which it was, really. "I'll make us some tea."

"Thank you. Can I help?"

"No need," he easily replied.

Dave put the kettle on, got the tea makings ready, and then took another couple of blankets over to the Cruiser. "Come on, you don't have to sit up there." Dave spread one of the blankets over the bonnet and windscreen, then indicated that Nicholas should get up there, make himself comfortable.

"Are you sure?" asked Nicholas.

"Absolutely. Go on. Just be careful of the windscreen wipers. Like, don't sit right on 'em, or anything."

"I won't. I know what this car means to you … Well, it's not a *car*, is it? This vehicle," he amended. And then he got it right: "Your beloved Cruiser."

Dave guffawed under his breath. "I'm that obvious, am I?"

"To someone who pays attention." Nicholas grinned unapologetically.

Dave didn't deign to respond. "I'll get the tea," he advised. Once they were both settled there on the bonnet, wrapped in blankets and with mugs of tea steaming from their hands, Dave said, "I remembered that story for you. About butterflies … ?"

Nicholas turned to him with the loveliest warmest smile.

Dave cleared his throat, and indicated the eastern horizon, which was starting to glow pale gold. "No, you watch the sunrise, and let me talk."

That lovely smile quirked with humour, and Nicholas turned away again. "All right."

"There's this Aussie singer–songwriter, Pete Murray. He's really good. I'll play you the CDs if you're interested."

"I'd love that," Nicholas murmured.

"Anyway, there's this song of his, called 'Ten Ft. Tall'. He tells the story behind it before he plays it at gigs. And it's about these two friends of his, who were childhood sweethearts. They grew up and got married, and were as happy as. She loved butterflies," Dave continued with a nod at Nicholas. "She always said that when she died, she'd come back as a butterfly."

Nicholas was silent now, staring towards the lightening sky, but also listening carefully.

"Well, she got cancer, though they were all still quite young. And she fought it for a couple of years, but eventually she passed away." He took a breath. "It was about a week after the funeral, her husband and his mates were having a quiet drink down the pub. It was already late, it was almost closing time. And this butterfly flew in through a window, and it headed right for the guy, and settled on his shoulder. And he didn't say anything. He just put down his beer and walked out of there. And the butterfly stayed with him the whole way home."

Nicholas was completely still. The gold grew brighter, and the sky overhead ran from blues, through rich purples, to black velvet.

"And Pete always finishes by saying that it's a true fact that butterflies never fly at night."

Silence.

"It's really awesome. I mean, it's an awesome part of the show. A great song."

Still nothing from Nicholas. Okay, something had evidently gone wrong somewhere.

"Mate –" Dave leaned forward to get a glimpse of Nicholas's face. And discovered that his eyes and cheeks were wet with tears. "Mate, you should have stopped me. It's a sad story, I know."

Nicholas glanced at him with a hint of that same lovely smile, only wobblier. "It's a beautiful story," he amended. "And you're a romantic, David Taylor!"

"I am not!" he retorted.

"No, of course not," Nicholas agreed, though with a catch in his voice. He'd turned away again, facing resolutely towards the sunrise, the breaking day. Either the sight was a distraction or it brought with it a man's fate, whether good or bad. "I'm sorry!" Nicholas said on a gasp. And, all right, obviously he was close to full–on weeping now.

"Ah, mate …" Dave reached to pat him on the back for sympathy, for reassurance.

And they sat there together watching the sky brighten, and then at last – suddenly – a molten line of gold appeared. Not so long after, the magic was chased away by the new clean day. Dave wasn't sure how much of that

Nicholas had managed to take in, but once it was over the man slipped away with another quiet apology, and disappeared into his tent.

Dave sighed, and went to brew more tea, and make breakfast.

five

The days and nights of the first week of their trip continued much the same. Except for the dawn tears; they avoided any repetition of that scene. Whenever Dave suspected that Nicholas was out there watching the sunrise, he just turned within his sleeping bag and went back to sleep for a while.

They got along well enough. Nicholas was engaged with his hunt, even though he was basically doing no more for now than providing further records for fairly well known phenomena. Dave was patient in assisting his client, and Nicholas was an efficient and uncomplaining member of Dave's camp.

The only time they came near to trouble was on the third evening, after Dave had checked in with Denise. Once he'd ended the call, he headed back towards his tent to put away the satellite phone – only to be met halfway there by Nicholas's puzzled scowl.

Dave almost stumbled a step, half surprised, half defensive.

"Are you going to call her *every* night?" Nicholas demanded.

"What? Yes."

"Seriously?"

"Yes. It's a matter of safety. Especially a trip like this when we don't know where we'll end up. I told you, she makes a note of the latitude and longitude, so –"

"I understand that."

So they'll know where to find the bodies. But of course he wasn't mean or unprofessional enough to say that. "Used to be Dad I'd call as often as Denny. Before he – you know. Died."

"But *every* night?" Nicholas returned, as if pleading for reason.

The defensiveness abruptly switched to its opposite. "*My* rules, remember? Life and death? You might be thankful some day that I was careful. Even," he allowed, the anger turning feeble already – "even a bit more careful than I needed to be."

"I think you're using that as an excuse."

Dave's head went back, and a stunned moment welled between them. Then he bit. "What if I am? What's your problem? Jealous, are you?"

Dave regretted that the moment it was out, but Nicholas responded quickly enough, as if he didn't see it as inappropriate at all. "Whether I am or not, I should think that any of your friends would be wanting you to move on by now – more than a *year* after she left you behind."

"Well," Dave started. "Look, she –" But he trailed off.

What could he say? How could he argue with a truth that no one else but for Denise herself had quite dared to tell him.

He took refuge in a rule that he should have remembered before now. "I appreciate your concern," Dave said frostily, "but it's none of your business. Just like your private life is none of mine."

"Right," Nicholas crisply responded, and he glared before turning away.

Still, half an hour later they were eating dinner across the campfire from one another, and they were conversing – a bit stiltedly, but with goodwill. And eventually in a quiet moment, Nicholas murmured, "I'm sorry, David."

"Not a problem," answered Dave. "I was out of line, too."

And he was rewarded with one of Nicholas's beautiful gentle smiles.

The real trouble began at the end of the week. Dave had begun packing up the camp as usual, but instead of pitching in as he always did, Nicholas was loitering, looking dissatisfied.

"I want to stay," Nicholas eventually announced.

"What?"

"I want to stay here at the campsite."

"No. No, we agreed. Once a week –"

"Supplies, I know. But you can go, can't you, David? You've gone alone for petrol and water before."

"Only once!" Dave slid one of the packing cases home into the back of the Cruiser, and then turned to consider the man. "It's not just supplies. It's civilisation. It's other people, and a proper bed for the night, and a proper meal. It's the news, and the internet, and calling home. Aren't you tired of my company yet?"

It was the wrong question, of course. Nicholas put his head down, but tilted one of his wicked little smiles up at Dave from under the brim of his Akubra. He really knew how to work that damned hat already. "No, I'm not tired of you yet. Maybe not ever."

"Right. Well. Don't you think your father would appreciate it if you emailed your butler or whatever, and told him you're still alive?"

Surprisingly, that earned him another scowl. "God, will you stop calling him that?"

"Who? Your father … ?"

"My butler *or whatever*," Nicholas returned mockingly. "I suppose you think you're being all very egalitarian, but I don't see why you should disapprove of someone getting paid well to do a good day's work. He helps us run that massive old house, which is trickier than you'd think, and he's been part of the family since before I was even born."

"All right!"

"And his *name*, which you'd know if you'd been paying attention, is Simon."

"Yes. All right. Simon. I had a fair bit to do with Simon while he was booking this trip, and I reckon he'd like to know you're alive."

"So, *you* can email him, can't you?"

Dave guffawed. "I think he expects more from me than to leave you alone at a campsite out the back of Bourke …"

Nicholas glared at him stubbornly, with his hands shoved hard into his jeans pockets. "I'll be all right. What's going to happen? Nothing bad has happened all this week!"

"It's no use pushing your luck," Dave advised. He could just imagine Nicholas blundering about: tripping over his own feet, hitting his head on something as he got back up, and God knows what after that. "Any one of a hundred things could go wrong, it could get really dire, and it would be my fault for leaving you here."

"David –"

"No, I can't do it."

"Can't or won't … ?"

"Both!"

"David, I might never get back here. I want to make the most of it."

"You've got to know when to quit, mate."

"The simple truth is that I *like* it out here. I want to have a day of peace and quiet out here, instead of –"

"No." Dave cut him off, and walked closer to make his point. "I *can't*, Nicholas. And what I say goes, remember? You promised me you'd respect that."

"For heaven's sake … I'm not asking for much."

"You're asking for far too much. You said you'd trust me."

"David –"

"Mr Goring –"

Nicholas let out an unhappy "Hah!" and turned away. A silence stretched, which Dave was wise enough not to break. "All right. If you're going to *Mr Goring* me, I'll have to take you seriously."

"Thank you."

"Under protest."

Dave sighed. "Would you please pack your bag? I need to take your tent down."

"Of course," said Nicholas quietly. "I'll help."

But that was only the beginning of it.

It was a different town, somewhat rougher than Charleville. Dave had friends there, but he thought of it as more frontier than civilisation. Still … in this day and age, he hadn't thought there'd be anywhere he maybe should think twice about taking Nicholas.

They arrived mid–afternoon, checked into a motel, took their accumulated garbage to the tip, and then went shopping. Nicholas came along, determined to help, despite Dave excusing him from any further responsibilities. Then while Dave was repacking the Cruiser with their new supplies, and filling up with water and petrol, Nicholas went to use the motel's Wi–Fi to connect to the internet.

"I'll say good day to Simon for you," Nicholas said over his shoulder as he headed off.

"Uh, that's *g'day*, thanks, mate."

"What*ever*."

Dave snorted. They were fine.

And they *were* fine together, as they ate dinner in the cafe attached to the motel. It was only when they went down to the town's pub in the evening that disaster struck.

"Day!" someone cried as the two of them walked in.

"Oh God," Dave muttered as he looked around for the source. If the guys were already drunk enough to not even bother with *Dave*, then they were well ahead and no doubt closing in on the finish line. "Hey," he greeted the little knot of boozed–up blokes off to the right of the bar. "How ya goin'?"

"Day maaaaate!" was the response, and "Taaay!" Someone managed his full name: "Day Taaay …"

"That good, then?" Dave queried, glancing back apologetically at Nicholas – who was looking unimpressed, and also a bit weary, as if he'd seen it all before. And surely blokes were blokes the world over, when they were stupid, young and drunk. "What ya' all up to?" Dave asked.

"Celebratin', Daaay! Ce–le–brate–*in*'!"

"Excellent." He didn't see any point in asking what, if anything, had been the excuse for such a session. No doubt he'd get the whole story later. "Right, well, don't let us interrupt you. I'll see ya later."

Unfortunately, however, one of them was still capable of adding two and two together and saying something coherent about it. "Day," the bloke said urgently. "Dave mate."

Dave turned back with a discreet sigh. "Um, yes?"

"Is this –" the man indicated Nicholas, with a wild gesture that slopped beer everywhere. "Is this the English poof, then?"

"Um, *earl*," Dave promptly supplied. "I'm pretty sure I said English *earl*."

"For heaven's sake," Nicholas muttered at his shoulder.

Dave was dying a little inside.

"Semantics," the drunk bloke observed dismissively.

"My, what big words you know," Dave returned, trying to turn it all into a bit of harmless banter. Because he knew these morons would only take such things so far. They might be obnoxious, but they weren't dangerous.

But it was too late. The mood had gotten edgier – and Nicholas had already walked away.

"Thanks, guys," Dave said flatly. "Thank you so much. Apart from anything else, *he's a client*."

"Awww, poor Day squiring around his English poof …"

"Not to mention he's a human being, you Neanderthals!"

They were too far gone to care, of course. Dave turned away, and followed Nicholas to the bar, relieved that at least Nicholas still seemed willing to have a drink there.

Although he might soon change his mind, given that the guys were calling after them, "Sorry, we don't serve iced Chardonnay here!" and,

"Maybe there's some sherry put by for the laaa–dies."

Nicholas was tense with anger, but he had both hands on the edge of the bar, all lined up to order, and when Dave reached his side, Nicholas half–turned to inform Dave with a terse politeness, "They have Cascade on tap."

"Great. That'll be great, thanks, mate." Dave cleared his throat, and before the barman got close, he offered, "Look, those idiots –"

"– are idiots. I know. Forget it."

And maybe that would have been that, if the drunken mob hadn't gotten it into their sodden heads to serenade Dave and Nicholas with a rousing chorus of 'Tiptoe Through the Mulga'.

"Right," said Nicholas. "I'll put up with five minutes of that, but not a whole evening."

"They won't last long. Short attention spans."

But Nicholas shook his head. "I'll see you back at the motel."

"Nicholas –"

But the man was already walking out, deliberately ignoring the idiots who were now going on about someone getting his knickers in a knot. And Dave, of course, followed Nicholas out, which prompted hoots about lovers' tiffs.

And then it was over, thank Christ, and Dave was out in the cool night air, with Nicholas striding on ahead with those long legs of his which obviously had far more power to them than Dave might have supposed. Dave didn't call out, but simply followed the man, and finally caught up with him as Nicholas's long pale fingers stuttered with the key at his motel room door.

Nicholas was furious and rightly so, but Dave could see that under the anger there was part of him that was simply hurt – and worse, a bit shamed. The man glanced up, startled and even scared for a moment, until he saw it was only Dave at his side. Nicholas glared at him defiantly. But when Nicholas dropped his gaze away then all Dave could see were those perfect plump lips and how they trembled. And he was pretty sure that if Nicholas were feeling any more confident, if he were at home and not alone round the other side of the world, he would have taken any teasing in good part and given back as good as he got – no doubt better.

"Those idiots," Dave quietly offered, "shouldn't have said any of that. But they *are* all talk, I can promise you that."

"What," Nicholas returned, in a low voice but still with a tremor, "so I shouldn't feel humiliated?"

"They're not worth it. You know you have nothing to feel bad about."

"David – I might never –"

The words halted and the man's head was still down, but Nicholas had turned back towards him, as if there was something he desperately needed to explain.

And the thing was – The thing was – Even if those blokes were mostly harmless, it had still been a horrible experience for Nicholas, and totally undeserved. And the thing was – Dave so wanted to make it up to him, to make him smile again. And the thought of surprising him out of it was a good one, too.

The moment stretched.

Then Dave leaned in and pressed his mouth to Nicholas's. Just for a heartbeat or two. The other man was startled, still. But then he pressed back for a beat. Not deepening it into a real kiss. Not pushing any further. Just returning the gesture. A grateful wistful smile was Dave's reward when he pulled back a moment later.

"Now," said Dave, all brisk yet friendly business. "I want you to get in there," he said, indicating the motel room, "and you'll be fine, but I want to hear you lock the door," he took a step back, in the direction of his own room, "because I want to know you're safe for the night and that you *feel* safe, too – and then I'll see you tomorrow morning for breakfast."

Nicholas was watching him back away with a hint of amusement twisting his lovely smile. He even let out a breath that might have almost been a laugh. "Thank you, David," he said. "Good night."

And then Nicholas slipped inside, and Dave waited to hear the lock clunk and the chain rattle into place, and then he turned and headed for his own room. And really, he thought he'd handled that quite well. He was quite pleased with himself, actually. Points for creativity, definitely. Nicholas was happier, and would hopefully sleep well. Everything was fine.

Except that Dave's heart was tripping over just a little too fast, and he was almost afraid to sleep for fear of what dreams might come.

six

They were quiet on the drive back out into their search area. Dave was conscious of Nicholas sitting peaceably beside him, tall yet comfortable in the passenger seat, still looking about him, happily engaged with all there was to experience out here.

Dave could hardly not be conscious of Nicholas, but mostly he was also paying great attention to the Cruiser. They had spent most of the previous week on sealed roads, but they were going to start exploring the dirt tracks now. There had been no sign of blue clouds or unknown waterholes so far, but it was early days – and Dave even reckoned it would be rather an anticlimax to find Nicholas's blues too quickly. Sometimes it wasn't all about the destination. Even Dave knew that.

The Cruiser handled beautifully, of course. She was going to be such a pleasure over the years …

"Yes, I'm sure you'll be very happy together," Nicholas murmured with a quirk of a smile.

"What?" He hadn't said anything out loud, had he?

"You're not the first man I've known who was in love with his car."

Dave cast him a sidelong look. "Not your chauffeur …"

"The same. Our family has a Rolls Royce Silver Cloud he held a deep affection for, but his real passion was for –"

"You."

Nicholas went pink about the cheeks, but otherwise ignored this gibe. "– an MGB V8 roadster in British Racing Green." A breath whistled out. "I was dead jealous, but I could see what he loved about her."

Dave laughed. "How very reasonable of you."

"He'd take me for a spin of an afternoon, if I'd been good."

"Good at what?"

"Oh shut up!" Nicholas cried, spluttering with laughter. "You ought to watch out, teasing me like that. I'll tell you all the graphic details if you're not careful."

"Quaking in my boots here."

"You should be," Nicholas advised darkly.

Dave just grinned at him, unrepentant. It seemed they were absolutely fine.

"I received a couple of very shamefaced phone calls this afternoon," Denise said when Dave called her that evening.

"Ah, you did, did you?"

"From your mates out at Woop Woop."

"Good. Though I'm amazed they even remember, to be honest."

"Still have a few brain cells intact, apparently." Denise was mystified. "What on earth did they say? I don't think I've ever heard a bloke sound so apologetic."

"Oh, it was nothing much. But they wouldn't let it go. It wasn't great, but Nicholas is all right about it now."

"If you take him back there, I'm sure they'll be suitably embarrassed to the point where even he won't be able to stand it. And no doubt they'll shout you all night, if you want."

Dave laughed. "Last thing we need is another drunken encounter with that lot. But I'll pass on their apologies."

"Think about it. It'll do them good to make amends."

"Well, maybe in a while. I think Nicholas was more … upset with himself for letting it matter."

"I get that," Denise said. "All right, well, if there's no other news I'll sign off, all right?"

"Talk to you tomorrow, Denny."

"Tomorrow, mate. Stay safe."

And they did indeed stay safe. The Cruiser performed admirably – though, after all, it wasn't exactly challenging terrain for her. The tracks occasionally passed through that fine sand that lesser vehicles sank into, and some tracks were beginning to lose the fight against the encroaching scrub, but Dave found his way through easily enough. His only concern was with the inbuilt satnav, which would occasionally flicker, lose its bearings, and then regroup, but Dave figured that was probably just to do with patchy satellite coverage out here. And it did always regroup. And if the worst came to the worst, he had a good old–fashioned paper map and a real compass packed safely away in the back.

Nicholas continued happily recording anything butterfly–related. They found a group of golden–winged butterflies fluttering about that afternoon, and Nicholas was soon taking notes and photos, his frown of concentration combining oddly with his delighted grin.

Dave watched him, assisting when required. "What do you call a group of butterflies, anyway? You know, like a pride of lions or whatever."

"A kaleidoscope of butterflies," Nicholas informed him, with a quirk of a brow.

"Seriously?"

"I kid you not. Perfect, isn't it? Here," he added, handing his gear over to Dave. "Just be still for a few minutes." And Nicholas stood there near the butterflies with his arms lifted a little, waiting.

"What are you … ?"

"Ssshh …" Nicholas threw him a grin, and then quieted again. And soon enough the butterflies drew near, and started to settle on his skin, on his forearms, and a couple of braver ones on his throat and the hint of chest left bare by his undone shirt buttons. Nicholas was looking as beatific as St Francis on a particularly grouse day.

Well, there was only one thing to do – once Dave had stopped grinning back at the man, of course. He slowly and quietly put everything down except Nicholas's camera, and then started taking photos. A few full–length shots, and then close–ups of the butterflies, and of that beatific beaming smile.

"Here," said Nicholas after a while. "I want some of you."

Dave scoffed a bit, but he was happy enough to let Nicholas have what he wanted. The man approached, pacing evenly, and encouraged one of the butterflies on his arm to shift over to Dave's instead. The thing tickled there, so beautiful and so delicate. Dave watched it, mesmerised, until the click and whirr of the camera shutter caught his attention, and he offered Nicholas a genuine smile to save in pixels.

Now that Nicholas was moving about, the butterflies had mostly lifted away to hover around him, but a few had come to Dave instead. They seemed to be – He carefully lifted an arm to look closer at one. It seemed to be smelling him, or something, with a long probing thing unwinding from just below its head to poke and dab at him. "What's he doing?"

"Drinking your sweat," Nicholas said, in tones that were amused and – it was true – slightly envious.

"Huh. Old pervs, the lot of you," Dave retorted, though more fondly than he'd intended.

Nicholas laughed, and went to sit in the chairs Dave had set beside the Cruiser. "Oh, he's not old. He's newly emerged. And the longest any butterfly has been known to live is eleven months. They know all about seizing the day. They have to!"

"They're gorgeous, aren't they?" Dave offered.

"Yes." Nicholas's smile was back. He picked up his guide, and quickly flipped through to a particular chapter. "Now, let's figure out exactly what he is …"

"I had another phone call for you today," Denise said that evening.

"What, *more* apologies? It's all coming back to them now, is it?"

"No, not that lot. A client. A potential client. D'you think you'll be with your earling for the full three months?"

"Well, I hope so."

A beat of silence.

Dave wondered what on earth he'd just said.

"Do you?" Denise belatedly asked. "I thought you were pretty much dreading it."

"No, it's fine, he's – great. Anyway, hopefully he'll find what he's looking for, and get the chance to study it properly, and –"

"And you like him, don't you?"

"Not like *that!*"

Denise just laughed. "Davey, I wasn't even going there, but seeing as you raised the topic …"

"Oh shut up," he grumbled without an ounce of heat.

"All right, well, I'll tell this guy you're definitely booked for the three months, but you're available after that. He's heard good things about you, Davey. I'm guessing he'll try to reschedule for later in the year."

"Okay, thanks, Denny, that's great." But he found himself watching Nicholas set the campfire, and when he wandered over there after putting the phone away, Dave met Nicholas's affectionate smile with one of his own.

That night, as they sat around the campfire, they weren't around it so much as by it. Because Nicholas had placed his chair close beside Dave's. Well, not *close* close but not far away either. And then Nicholas sat there. With his forearm resting on the chair arm, and his long hand with its pale fingers dangling from that narrow wrist. And he very deliberately *didn't* reach to hold Dave's hand. Dave was watching him warily from the very edges of his gaze, and he could see that Nicholas was holding himself back, almost as if the sheer anticipation of the chance that he *might* cross that boundary was the most delicious thing out.

For once they didn't talk much. Until at last Dave thought it was better to clear matters up now rather than risk any misunderstandings. Because it seemed that, quite inadvertently, and to be honest he really wasn't sure how, Things Had Taken A Turn.

"Look," said Dave into the silence. "Nicholas." Staring hard at the flames dancing on the wood.

"Mmm … ?" said Nicholas in response.

"I'm *not* homophobic. That's not where this is coming from. But I'm *not* gay."

"I think that –"

Dave barrelled on regardless. "It doesn't matter to me that you like men. Honestly. I always thought that it didn't matter whether you loved a guy or a girl. What matters is that you love the *person*. You are in love with the person."

Nicholas was watching him with a guarded kind of interest. "So why can't your person be a guy?"

That flummoxed him. Dave thought about it. "Denny," he said after a while. "There's Denise."

"I know you loved her," Nicholas said, expansive. Reasonable. "You're loyal enough to love her still, which is not such a deal–breaker as your friend in Toowoomba seems to think. But I think you could feel that way for a guy as well. I think if you met the right person, it wouldn't matter whether they were a guy or a girl."

"Well, I guess that's true in a general kind of way –"

"Oh come on!" Nicholas cried. "It's not about theory, it's about practice."

"But I don't –"

"You *kissed* me."

Dave frowned, and wondered if the night's darkness would hide the fact he'd just turned pale. "I did," he admitted. "But just to, like … cheer you up."

"Right …"

"It's not as if it was a real kiss."

Nicholas was merciless with the light scepticism. "You can tell yourself that, David, if it helps you sleep at night."

"Well, that doesn't make a difference, anyway, does it? A guy or a girl. It's still a kiss. It's not like – their bits are involved."

Nicholas laughed hollowly. "Oh, my boy bits got involved, believe me."

Dave threw him a scowl, but then frowned as he tried to think it through. "It's not something I've done before," he eventually continued. "In fact, I've only ever been with Denise. That'll sound pathetic to you, I'm sure, but I've never even kissed anyone else."

The tones in response to this confession were a little softer. "Then I'm honoured, and I'm glad. Thank you, David." After a moment, Nicholas argued as strongly as ever, "But that puts me in a category that consists of only two people in all the world. And I say that a kiss isn't just a kiss. Apart from which, you called me beautiful."

Dave went from pale to bright red in a millisecond. "I did not!"

"You did, too. You were driving at the time. At first I thought you were murmuring sweet nothings to the Cruiser. But you weren't." Nicholas grimaced a little. "I suspect I wasn't meant to hear. You seemed to be thinking out loud."

"Oh."

"Ha! So you're not denying that you've thought it."

"Well –"

"Obviously you have atrocious taste, but in this particular case I'm not going to argue you out of it."

"Look," Dave finally came back at the man with. "Just because I said – I mean, you are, that's all, and I can have an objective opinion, can't I? I can think that guys are beautiful in a purely es – esth –"

"Aesthetic."

"Thank you. – sense. I can appreciate a guy like I'd appreciate … a sunrise!"

"Right. Especially one you've kissed."

"Oh God, shut up, would you?"

"I just don't think that straight guys *think* like that."

"Well, obviously they do. It's self–evident! Cos here I am, thinking like that."

Nicholas was about to retort, but then he seemed to have second thoughts, and closed his mouth again. A moment went by, before Nicholas sighed, and asked, "Why are you fighting this?"

"What! Why are *you*?"

"Because I fancy you, of course! I've fancied you since the moment I saw you at the airport. I fell at your feet, remember?"

"You tripped on the trolley."

"You distracted me, all fit and golden–haired and *beyond* handsome, like some Australian god …"

Dave had no words in response to any of that.

"Since then, I've got to know you a bit. And I like you, David. Very much. I like you very much."

"Well, and I like you," Dave was able to say, "but that doesn't mean –"

"All right, all right!" Nicholas lifted his hands with palms out, as if giving up at last. Or maybe he just couldn't bear to hear any more. "I'm sorry. I'll let you be. Of course I don't want you feeling harassed. I just thought –"

"What? What did you think?"

"That we might have a chance."

Dave looked at him, and saw the very real emotion that was barely hidden by a cool exterior shell. And for the first time in a very very long time, he used the S word. "I'm sorry, mate," he murmured.

And Nicholas quietly replied, "I am, too."

Nicholas seemed to take this final rejection philosophically. He didn't get angry, he didn't sulk. He didn't even get sad, though his happiness felt a shade less bright. Dave found himself missing those hundred–watt grins, though he could hardly change things back to how they were when it had been based on a misunderstanding. He was scrupulous in continuing to be as professional a guide and as friendly a host as he always was, though, and

Nicholas likewise continued to be the perfectly equable and helpful client. Perhaps they didn't talk quite as much, but that was all.

And one thing they definitely didn't talk about was the next trip to town.

Dave got up early that day, only to find that Nicholas had gotten up earlier, and was already brewing a pot of tea. Nicholas was sitting on one of the chairs, slumped down into it with a blanket wrapped around his shoulders. And he had his stubborn face on.

"Morning," said Dave.

"Good morning, David," was the reply, more formal than ever.

After dealing with the necessaries, Dave came back and sat in the chair near Nicholas's. Accepted a mug of tea. "Well?" he prompted once the tea was cool enough for him to take a reviving mouthful or two.

"I'm not coming into town with you, David. Not this time."

"My rule still holds."

"I think you can make an exception."

"I'm concerned for your safety. Anything might happen. And you haven't learned enough in two weeks to know how to survive out here."

Nicholas looked across at him, and said very reasonably, "I'm not going. I'm sorry, but I'm not."

Dave let a moment or two drift by. He drank some more tea. He sighed. "We're not going to have a repeat of last week's dramas. You might have noticed, I've been taking us generally north–east. I figured we'd go to Charleville. Nothing bad happened there, did it? And if Charlie's there … Well, he knows who you are, and he welcomed you."

Nicholas nodded soberly. "I shall miss seeing Charles again. But I'm going to stay here. I'm sorry, David," he said again.

For a long while – through that cuppa, and then a second one – a silence stretched, and Dave thought about the situation. Well, he didn't really think about it as such, but instead reflected on an inevitability that didn't make him happy at all. It seemed that Nicholas was determined to have his way. And while the professional David Taylor could pull rank and overrule him, the soft–hearted Davey knew that he was already too involved with this man to do so. But that left Dave making a decision that he knew was wrong, that he already felt bad about.

He thought some more.

"All right," David eventually agreed after Nicholas had quietly gone about setting up breakfast for them both. "All right, you can stay. But I'll only go for the day. I'll be back for dinner."

"You don't have to give up your night in town for my sake."

"But I do," Dave explained in simple tones. "There is absolutely no way I'm going to leave you alone out here overnight. Just *no* way."

"But –"

"No, Nicholas. I'm not happy about this anyway. You've drawn your line, and you're just gonna have to let me draw mine."

Nicholas was staring at him with those deep dark eyes, and there was a storm happening in there, even if the surface was calm. They sat there at the foldout table, neither of them eating. "David, I didn't mean to make you –"

"If I could live my life without rules," Dave blurted, "that'd be great. Well, you know, not without decency, and Do Unto Others, and all that. But out here – you won't live long if you're not careful. There's a reason for every single one of my rules. There really is."

"I know, David. I understand they're not arbitrary."

"So don't go thinking that cos I gave in on this one, I'll start giving in on others. It can't work like that."

"I won't ask for anything else," Nicholas promised. He sounded almost as if he wished he hadn't even asked for this. "I'll come in with you, if you insist. If we both go for the day –"

"No," said Dave, bitterly. Stupidly. "No, you stay, if that's what you really want."

The turmoil was visible on Nicholas's face now. "David –" He reached to rest a cool palm and long fingers against Dave's hand where it lay on the table.

Dave withdrew his hand, and went to fetch the satphone. "I've shown you how to use this. Do you remember?"

"Yes, David."

"The first number programmed in is Denise, and the second is Charlie. I've put my mobile number in, too, now; it's the seventh one. But if you need me, I don't care what for, and you can't get through to me, then call Charlie. If you can't get hold of him, then call Denise. She'll know what to do. All right?"

"Yes, David," Nicholas humbly agreed.

"And you do what they tell you to, even if it makes no sense to you. Even if you don't want to."

"Yes, David."

"You promise? And I mean it. Call about anything. Even if it's just that you can't decide whether to have baked beans or spaghetti with meatballs for lunch."

That won a smile from the man. "I promise. And I appreciate what you're doing. Very much."

"I'm an idiot," Dave said, angry with himself, but unaccountably fond of the man who was making him so idiotic.

"You're the most amazing man in all the world."

"Huh," said Dave. And he went to fetch his shopping list. When he emerged from his tent, he found Nicholas waiting with a thermos of coffee for him. "Well," he had to admit in a mutter, "you're not too shabby yourself."

Dave was out of sorts all day, and he knew well enough why. He'd not only done the wrong thing but he'd done it for the wrong reason. Underneath which was a low–level, fairly realistic buzz of anxiety that he knew wouldn't quieten until he saw Nicholas again, whole and safe.

His thoughts were in a constant fret, going over and over all the advice he'd passed on. *Don't wander so far that the camp's out of sight. You'll get turned around, and head off in the wrong direction, and you'll be lost. Don't leave uncovered food or water out. You'll attract the wrong kind of attention. Don't –* And so on, and so on. How much of it Nicholas had actually taken in was another matter entirely. Dave hoped he wouldn't find that out the hard way.

Charlie came to find him at the grocery store. "I heard you were in town again."

"Just for the day, mate."

After a brief glance around, Charlie asked, "Where's your man, Davey?"

"Nicholas is *hardly* my man."

"Bring him down the pub for lunch. It'll be good to see him again."

"I can't," Dave said. And then he explained why.

"Come anyway, mate. You need to talk."

"I've never done anything stupider," Dave announced once their meals were served. He didn't really feel like eating, though he always looked forward to having a proper meal in town.

"He'll be all right," said Charlie.

"How do you know?" Dave asked, searching Charlie's cheerfully worn face, hoping for even a mystical Dreamtime kind of reassurance – the sort of thing that he wouldn't really believe, but which would feel comforting.

"I have faith … that this isn't Nicholas's fate."

"Faith?" Dave sighed. Faith seemed like little more than blind belief to him. "Do you *know* what a clumsy bugger he is? If anyone could –" He forced himself not to imagine any more disastrous scenarios. "I should never have let him talk me into it."

"Don't be so hard on yourself."

"Someone has to be," Dave said darkly.

Charlie considered him silently for a time, in between mouthfuls of steak, spud and veg. Eventually the man observed, "You care about him, Davey."

"Course I do," he replied a bit scornfully. "I know he's a bit – odd. Nothing like what I expected. But he's become a mate."

"Of course he has," Charlie quietly agreed. "He'll be fine today. And I know you'll take good care of him. But you need to take better care of yourself as well, Davey."

"Uh huh," Dave neutrally agreed around a mouthful of steak.

"How goes the quest for Nicholas's butterflies?"

Dave rolled his eyes. "Nothing. Well, just the sort of grubs and butterflies you'd expect to find, apparently. Which he's happy enough about, and he's busy gathering all the data he can. But no blue clouds, no mysterious waterholes – nothing that's never been seen before."

Charlie nodded for a moment, sagely. "The time has to be right."

"Right time in the right place. I get that. The distances we're covering each day, we're giving ourselves every chance to stumble into it."

"Mmm." Charlie sat back, and mused over his beer. "There's … a strangeness down around there. There's a mystery."

"Right …" Dave warily agreed, wondering if he dared prompt Charlie for more information – or if Dave might even be better off not muddling his head with half–hints of Dreamtime secrets.

"It's reasonable to assume you're not gonna find it the regular way."

"Mmm …"

"Maybe – you have to *not* want to find it."

"What?"

Charlie shrugged. "Maybe you have to *not* be looking."

"How does that work, then?"

Another shrug, and Charlie's gaze slid away.

Dave sighed. Sometimes he reckoned he was just a bit too white and ordinary for the Outback.

As Dave drove back to the camp, the Cruiser's satnav began doing that odd flickering and resetting thing again. Which didn't help his peace of mind, though he had a good sense of direction, and reckoned he could almost certainly find the camp again just on his own instincts. It was a bit of a worry, though, and no doubt he should try to have someone look at it before he and Nicholas really went off–road.

His thoughts were nothing but fretful as the sun started westering. But soon enough he saw the camp in the distance across the flat landscape, and at last he could make out Nicholas standing there waiting for him, and Nicholas appeared to be upright and in one piece, so maybe everything had quite unexpectedly turned out fine. After long moments Dave tore his gaze off that long tall figure in his Akubra and sage green shirt and blue jeans – tore his gaze away to glance across what he could see of the camp, which all seemed to be in much the same state he'd left it that morning. So maybe everything really was fine.

In those last moments before he parked the Cruiser, Dave was abruptly swamped with fury – the sort unleashed in a parent the moment after their child is safe and the danger is past. *What did you think you were DOING?! How could you have been so STUPID?!* But then that ebbed away, too, and Dave was left with a giddy sense of relief, and he knew he was grinning like a loon as he finally turned off the ignition and climbed out of the Cruiser. He approached Nicholas, his grin only broadening even while he felt more and more idiotic – and Nicholas stood there with his hands jammed into his jeans pockets, his grin just as wide as Dave's, and he was kind of shifting about on his feet as if he couldn't quite keep still but he was forcing himself not to – well, not to just grab Dave and hug him, Dave imagined.

"So," said Dave. "You managed not to lose a limb or set fire to your tent or anything?"

"Seems like it," Nicholas agreed. "But I –"

"But you what?" Dave prompted after a pause, though somehow he knew it wasn't anything serious.

Nicholas had his mouth pressed tightly closed, and just shook his head to indicate he wasn't saying anything further for fear of incriminating himself.

Dave had a stab at it. "But you missed me."

Those lips remained pressed together, but widened and quirked into a flat version of the man's wicked grin, while his deep blue eyes danced and his shoulders quivered with laughter.

"You're never going to stay behind again."

Nicholas shook his head emphatically. *Never.*

"Good," said Dave. He let his smile turn affectionate for a moment, risking the man reading that as *I missed you, too.*

And indeed Nicholas's lips parted on a silent huff, and then turned sweetly poignant …

Oh God, thought Dave, *and there's another of The Thousand Smiles of Nicholas Goring. Why on earth hasn't he found a man yet who can see the wisdom of devoting a life to cataloguing them all?*

Nicholas was standing there with his hands hanging free now, standing there so very still, watching Dave. Hardly even breathing, apparently.

It was the first time that Dave had been conscious he might actually be in some danger here. *When did that happen?* he asked himself. *And how?*

There was no answer, of course. The moment lengthened as they considered each other; Nicholas waiting, and Dave's brow beginning to wrinkle with puzzlement.

But Dave soon cleared his throat and turned away. "Right. Groceries. Let's get these unpacked and stowed," he said, heading around the back of the Cruiser. "And then I got one of Billy's homemade meat pies for our dinner. To celebrate, you know?"

"Celebrate?" Nicholas asked in a neutral tone. He was standing there beside him now, uncomplainingly letting Dave load him down with grocery bags.

"Celebrate, yeah. My safe return. You being whole and well. The camp not being destroyed."

Nicholas nodded, as if still not quite trusting himself to speak.

Dave was the opposite, though, babbling on and unable to stop himself even though he knew it was just an avoidance tactic. "So we can continue enjoying our inalienable rights," he said.

Warily, Nicholas asked, "Which would be … ?"

"Life, liberty, and the pursuit of butterflies, of course. What else?"

Nicholas guffawed quite happily, and they were all right again. They were fine. Everything felt easy between them. Nothing need change.

Even though Dave was visually charting Nicholas's post–guffaw contentment, and thinking, *One thousand and one*.

seven

During their third week, they decided, they'd concentrate on trying to find the waterhole where the Barcoo grunter ancestor was dreaming through his long sleep. They had historical maps as well as current ones, and Dave had worked out an itinerary that took in any water feature whatsoever, whether it still existed or not. If that didn't work, they would start exploring any ground at lower levels. The landscape appeared quite flat, but it wasn't really; there were gradual rises and falls, there were folds and creases between them where any rare rainfall would collect and run off. The waterhole might be more myth than reality, but they had to try.

The search was disheartening, though. "I hadn't realised everything was so dry out here," Nicholas commented on the third afternoon, as Dave steered the Cruiser up out of a dent in the landscape and back onto an unsurfaced track. "Butterflies need liquid of some kind, almost *any* kind. It can be quite ghastly what they'll drink, but they need *something*."

"That goes for any living thing, doesn't it?"

"Well, it's just that adult butterflies only drink. They don't eat. But there aren't even any flowers out here for them to sip nectar from."

Dave had to laugh at that. "Sipping flower nectar doesn't sound so gross."

Nicholas cast him a dark glance. "We'll just leave that topic there, then."

"All right! Where to next?" he asked Nicholas, who was navigating from an armful of maps and the handwritten notes they'd both made.

Nicholas sighed, and traced their recent meanderings on the map with one of his long pale fingers. Dave tore his gaze away only just in time to avoid leaving the track and scratching the Cruiser against one of the older gnarled shrubs. It was only that he was interested in their route, of course. And it was only concern for the Cruiser and for their safety that caused his eyes to be drawn to Nicholas gently tapping a fingertip on the satnav, prompting it to reboot.

"That's been playing up again," Dave observed.

"It's as if something is interfering with the signal. Though I can't think what, out here."

Dave glanced at him. "You don't think it's just faulty?"

Nicholas gasped in mock horror. "How dare you! That's one of the

Cruiser's very own instruments you're maligning."

"Hah! I think they call that Stockholm Syndrome, don't they?"

"You'll be loving butterflies next," Nicholas supplied.

"They're beautiful!" Dave protested like a true convert. "What are you saying?"

Nicholas smiled a bit smugly, and left well enough alone. And afterwards Dave thought that maybe that was just as well, for God only knew what else Nicholas might convert him to.

"Do you think it's the satellite coverage?" Nicholas asked a few kilometres later. "I mean, maybe there aren't many that fly over this region."

"Yeah, though it hasn't been a problem before. There's always been enough."

"How about the phone? You're getting through to Denise every evening."

"So far. There were only one or two nights when that was a bit patchy, too."

Nicholas made a non-committal noise of agreement, and turned his attention back to the maps.

Another few kilometres passed, with no variation in the landscape. But they were almost at the top of a long rise now, so when they started heading down again, there would be something to explore.

"The thing I'm still wondering is," Dave said into the companionable silence, "how do you find a blue cloud in a blue sky?"

"It's beginning to seem rather impossible."

"What? No, don't give up yet!" He felt quite alarmed by this sudden turn into negativity.

"I only have so much time …" Nicholas observed, slowly and quietly.

"No, you haven't even been here three full weeks yet. You knew it might take a while. That was the whole idea of the three months, wasn't it?"

A silence stretched. The satnav flickered and went offline.

Then Nicholas said, "Maybe we want it too much. Maybe we have to *not* want to find it."

Dave looked at him askance. After a moment he admitted, "That's what Charlie said."

"What?"

"When I went up to Charleville the other day."

"Why didn't you tell me?"

"Because it makes no sense!"

"I don't care. Let's try it."

Dave rolled his eyes. But he also waited to hear what their next plan might be.

Nicholas sat there thinking furiously. "Maybe we have to let go of the *need*."

"And you could do that, could you? Quit needing your butterflies."

"If I have to."

Dave sighed. At this point, he'd try almost anything. "All right, sure. Let's stop trying. We're just driving along here for our amusement."

Nicholas said with a fair attempt at world–weariness, "I don't even care anymore. Who could possibly give a damn?"

"It was just an excuse for a holiday, right?"

"Right," Nicholas agreed. "Just an excuse to have you to myself for three months."

"Huh." The driest hint of an old creek bed appeared on either side of where the track cut through it. Dave's instincts were to turn right, so he turned left into it, with an odd feeling of abandon.

"Wait, that's the wrong way!" Nicholas cried out.

"There's no right or wrong," Dave argued. "It's not like we're looking for anything, is it? It's not like we're going any place in particular."

Nicholas grinned at him, and settled back in his seat again. "Of course." He looked idly around him, making a great show of not hunting anymore.

They continued on for a while, and Dave's concentration was all for the terrain; there were rocks occasionally, although the ground remained fairly even. But then they topped another slight rise, and there didn't seem to be a mirroring trace of old run–off on the other side. Dave paused for a moment, looking about him at this new territory, which seemed to be a wide shallow basin; the horizon was visibly nearer on every side than they'd been used to.

"Where –" Nicholas began, looking from the landscape to the maps and trying to match one to the other. "I can't quite –"

From the corner of Dave's eye as he scanned around again, he caught a glimpse of something. It was as if a tiny part of the sky had moved.

"What was that?" Nicholas asked in that very moment, in a hushed tone. He'd tensed up again as if an electric current had gone through him.

"What was what?" Dave asked – but his sudden testiness betrayed the fact that he'd seen it, too.

"Like a shimmer, or something."

"Heat haze," Dave said, dismissing the whole thing. But he had turned the Cruiser towards it, and they headed slowly down into the valley.

They were both staring ahead, trying to track a piece of sky that for much of the time looked like any other piece of sky, while Dave was also very conscious of steering the Cruiser safely through the scrub which was slightly denser here than it had been on the other side of the ridge.

"There!" Nicholas cried. "To the left a bit."

Dave corrected his course, having thought he'd glimpsed the flutter, too, even though he'd been mid–blink.

They continued silently on, not seeing any more evidence of whatever it was, but eventually reaching a strange place where a worn old watercourse led out from a sunken piece of ground. Dave brought the Cruiser to a halt a few metres away, and they sat there leaning forward in their seats to stare at this discovery.

It was hard to quite make it all out, but it seemed quite large, this valley within a valley – and there were larger shrubs and trees growing within it, though none of them grew so tall that they stood out from the surrounding scrub. If you were looking across the terrain, chances were you wouldn't even see it.

"I *scoured* Google Maps," Nicholas said in a hushed kind of awe. "The satellite images, you know?"

"It would have just looked like a denser part of the scrub," Dave affirmed.

"And there were a few areas where the images were a bit blurry, a bit odd ..." They both glanced again at the satnav, which seemed to have given up entirely. "Poor coverage," Nicholas tried.

"What you said before, about something interfering with the signal ..."

"Yes?"

"There are huge mineral deposits around here. Australia's known for them. It's such an old place, geologically. So, I was thinking, what if there's a lot of ... something like iron ore here. And it's jamming the signals."

"Is that possible?"

"I don't know. But it would help explain why this wasn't on any of the modern maps."

"It has to be," Nicholas weakly asserted, sitting back to shuffle through the maps again, though he knew as well as Dave that they were all empty around these parts. After a moment, he sat back up again. "Can we drive down into it?" And for once he was actually asking permission, and letting Dave decide, and knowing that Dave might refuse.

Dave thought for a while. And then turned off the ignition. Before Nicholas's face could fall, Dave said, "We'll walk in."

And Nicholas was suddenly just *glowing* with anticipation. This man who didn't think he was beautiful was just … glowing. And gorgeous.

"We'll leave the Cruiser out here," Dave said, trying to concentrate on practical matters. "Don't know what we'll find in there, and we can't afford to lose it or get it stuck."

"I understand."

"Not that she can't cope with a lot of different situations –"

"Of course," Nicholas stoutly agreed, laying a gently reassuring hand on the top of the dashboard.

"Anyway, if it comes to anyone sending out an aerial search team, she's much easier to spot than either of us – or that … whatever it is."

"It's the waterhole," breathed Nicholas.

"We don't know that yet."

Nicholas just looked at him. *Yes, we do.*

"The rule still holds. You do what I tell you. All right? If it's a sinkhole of some kind, if it's at all unstable, then we'll –"

"How can it be unstable, with those trees growing in it? It must be at least thirty or forty years old, judging by the size of those gum trees – and older still if it's what I think it is."

Dave just looked at him.

"Sorry," Nicholas said, with honest chagrin. "We'll take it slow, and I'll do what you tell me."

"All right," Dave agreed, with far more severity than he felt he had any claim to.

"Thank you, David."

"Let's go, then."

They paused on the brink of this strange place, to discover what might serve as a track curving down into it along the left wall, which was otherwise quite steep.

"How wonderful," marvelled Nicholas.

"It's bizarre," countered Dave, though he knew he sounded just as awestruck. He checked again that they had what they might need. There was a good length of rope in his backpack, along with a torch, the small first aid kit, and some food. Both he and Nicholas were carrying full water bottles. Chances were they'd need nothing but a refreshing drink once they were in there, but it was a foolish man who relied on chances in the Outback. "All right?" he asked Nicholas again, just in case.

An eager nod was the only reply. Nicholas had his satchel with him, trusting that he would have plenty of discoveries to record. And maybe Dave was just too caught up in the excitement, but he was feeling almost as certain as Nicholas was that they had finally found what they'd been looking for.

"Come on, then," Dave said. And they crossed the edge and walked down into this place, shoulder to shoulder.

Dave was evaluating the track as they went, of course. It seemed wide enough and solid enough for the Cruiser, apparently formed from a harder layer of sedimentary rock that hadn't been worn away yet. The strata that formed the cliff wall above them were reddish with occasional blackish streaks, which hinted at iron ore.

The track lowered them down into the small valley, with one twist that would require a three-point turn, before leaving them on a gently sloping floor. Then the main impediment for the Cruiser would be picking a way between shrubs and trees, but they weren't so closely packed that it couldn't be done.

The temperature was a couple of degrees cooler down here, and there was that crisp feel in the air of a body of water nearby. Nicholas cast Dave an excited look, but he kept pace with Dave, and didn't try to push ahead.

They followed the slope of the ground to eventually emerge from sparse undergrowth and find a pool of still water that was the most astonishing green–blue. The trees provided a light cover over it all, but sunlight dappled around them and sang glints of brightness off the water. It was … magical.

They stood there staring at the scene for a long while, dumbfounded at finding so much beauty that was so untouched. It seemed that nothing had been disturbed here for years, decades even. Dave couldn't even see any evidence of animals, though why they wouldn't use the only waterhole around for tens of kilometres, he couldn't begin to imagine.

As if Dave's thought of animals had triggered Nicholas's memory, the man cast him a querying look, and when Dave nodded permission, Nicholas looked about him and wandered back along the trees, searching. Dave trailed after him, watching Nicholas, but also glancing around, wanting to get a feel for their surroundings.

And it was Dave who spotted them first. "Flowers," he said – and then had to clear his throat before trying again. "You said they drink flower nectar, right?"

Nicholas looked up, and swung around to see where Dave was pointing. In a dell hidden beyond an ages–old rockfall, a cluster of wattle offered dark gold blooms to the sun. Nicholas gasped a little, and halted. Held out a hand to indicate they should tread carefully. That was all right. Dave knew the drill by now.

Slowly Nicholas approached the plants, bent almost double already to peer in amidst the foliage, keeping an eye on where he was walking. Dave followed him, not deviating from the path he'd set. Nicholas pushed his Akubra back, the better to see.

And then Nicholas had fallen to his knees by the nearest wattle, staring hard, his hands spread on his own narrow denim–clad thighs, fingers white with pressure. Dave waited, keeping his distance. But after long moments, Nicholas reached back, and then turned towards him, that long face both shocked and beatific. "We've found them," Nicholas whispered hoarsely.

"We have?" Dave took the hand that reached towards him, and let himself be gathered in. He crouched carefully just by Nicholas, though still keeping a little further back. He was trying to find blue wings, but couldn't see anything. "Where?" he asked, hushed. "What am I looking for?"

Nicholas laughed, sounding a little hysterical. "Don't you know a pupa when you see one by now? There –" He pointed carefully at … a pupa on a narrow branch of the wattle, that matched so precisely it all looked just like a bumpy branch. Unless you had it pointed out to you. "And there –"

"I see now …" There were heaps, now that Dave could identify them. "How do you know they're yours?"

Nicholas shot him a grin tinged with a delightful kind of madness. "I've never seen anything quite like them. But you're right. We need to make sure." He reached into his satchel for his camera, and took a few photos, carefully focussing in on the pupae. Then he shifted back and refolded to sit cross-legged, before pulling out his field guide and starting to leaf through it.

Dave settled himself in beside the man, and slipped off his backpack. This could take a while, he knew. He took out his water bottle, and swallowed a few mouthfuls; handed it to Nicholas, who did likewise; then Dave drank again. They were long past worrying about things like sharing utensils. Dave pondered that while Nicholas leafed through pages, muttering to himself about form, colour and texture; about tapering spinules, lateral flanges and anal hooks. Which Dave thought sounded rather painful.

"Sorry," Nicholas murmured, shooting Dave a mischievous glance. "That's how they attach themselves to the branches. Well, that or silken girdles!"

"That's so queer," Dave commented. "No wonder you're so fascinated." To which Nicholas just gave him a droll look, before returning to his book.

Occasionally Nicholas would hand Dave the guide and tip forward onto his hands and knees to peer in at a pupa. Sometimes he picked up his camera, and considered the photos on the digital display, zooming in close to see the details. Eventually he announced, "I'm not finding anything that matches."

"I believe you."

Nicholas laughed. "Sounding a bit defensive, am I? Well, I'll keep an open mind, I promise you that, and we won't know for sure until they transform into adults. But this is what I've been searching for, David. These are our butterflies!"

Dave just smiled at the man, and didn't even tease. *So much for an open mind, indeed!* But the last thing he could possibly want was to quench the light in those beautiful bright blue eyes.

Eventually Nicholas was done for now in poring over his bits of stick that weren't. With a sigh he unfolded, and lay back on the ground beside where Dave sat, closing his eyes to let the dappled sunlight bathe his face. After a moment one of his hands found Dave's, and those long fingers dovetailed with his own.

"We're just going to stay here now, aren't we?" Nicholas asked, obviously not dreading the answer.

"Yes. For as long as you need." Dave felt obliged to add, "Other than weekly trips for supplies."

"Of course. Do you think you can bring the Cruiser down into here?"

"Possibly," Dave allowed. When Nicholas opened one narrow eye to consider him, Dave provided a truer answer. "Yes, I could drive her down here, and get her back out again, I reckon. Easy. That's not the problem."

"What's the problem, then?" Nicholas tilted his head back to look at the flat and relatively empty area between the trees and the water. "I was hoping we could set up camp down here."

"I know."

"At least it's a bit cooler down here. It's got to be more comfortable. Quite apart from being close to the butterflies."

"Yes. I just don't know how wise it is."

"What could go wrong?"

"I don't know. That's the problem."

Nicholas lifted up onto his elbows to consider Dave. "Nothing's changed around here for years. Even the water level looks like it's stayed the same."

Dave nodded. "The pool must be fed from the water table."

"Well, then?"

Dave scrunched up his face, knowing he didn't have much to go on other than a sense of unease. "There's no trace of animals coming down here. And why wouldn't they? It's the only standing water in this whole area. No sign of birds inhabiting the trees."

"But our butterflies are protecting themselves from something. They're pretty well disguised."

"Maybe they just haven't bothered evolving. I don't know. Anyway," Dave added. "Charlie said –"

That had Nicholas sitting up beside him, looking a bit disgruntled for the first time. "*What* did Charles say? And what else haven't you told me?"

"Nothing. Nothing, really. He just talked about … a mystery. A strangeness."

"What did he mean?"

"I have no idea. I didn't want to push. I mean, he's obviously helped us a bit more than he should. We've found ourselves the Dreamtime place where the Barcoo grunter ancestor sleeps …"

"The old grunter knew what he was doing, didn't he?" Nicholas agreed with a laugh. "I can imagine worse places to spend eternity."

"Yeah, but I don't know whether Charlie was trying to warn me about something."

Nicholas thought about that for a long moment. Eventually he concluded, "No, Charles would have said if he thought we'd be in danger."

"They can be really secretive when it comes to Dreamtime stuff."

"Oh come on, he's your friend! There's no way he would have let us just walk into danger. He would have found some way of telling you. Or he would have sent us off in a different direction altogether."

"I suppose …"

"Well, then … ?"

Dave sighed. "Not tonight, Nicholas. Give me twenty–four hours. We'll camp up by the Cruiser tonight, and then tomorrow –"

"Yes?"

"We'll see."

Nicholas grinned at him. And then lifted Dave's hand – not to kiss it, thank God, but to caress Dave's palm with his cheek. Which was almost as bad. Maybe it was worse. "Thank you, David."

"Nnn," he said, quite coherently.

As the westering sun left the waterhole in an early twilight, Dave looked at Nicholas, and Nicholas simply said, "I know."

"There'll still be an hour of sunlight up there, but we'd better get the camp set up."

One of Nicholas's gentle smiles blessed him. "I know, David." He was already packing his camera and things back into his satchel. "I'm ready."

"I'm probably being paranoid, but I don't want you coming back down here alone. Not until we're sure."

Nicholas nodded. "I know. It's all right."

"Really?"

"You make the rules, David."

He thought to wonder how long that was going to last. And later on he was relieved, though he hardly admitted it even to himself, when Nicholas without question or remark set up the second tent as if it were still a matter of course.

That evening, Dave had to drive out to the furthest rim of the wider valley before he could get a signal on the satphone or a reading of their location off the satnav.

"We're settled here now," Dave said to Denise. "But I can't call you from our campsite. We must be in some kind of blind spot."

"All right. Just give me the directions from where you are now, in case." When he was done, Denise said, "That sounds pretty incredible."

"It is. But it's like no one's been down there for decades, if ever. It's kind of eerie."

"Beautiful, though."

"Yes. Very beautiful." He thought about that, and about how he *wanted* to feel uneasy while down there by the waterhole, but he couldn't. Not really. The place was weird, but it wasn't *wrong*. "Maybe the only problem is that it's almost too good to be true."

"You should just enjoy it," Denise advised.

"Maybe I should."

"Look, d'you wanna just call me next time you're in town? I won't panic if I don't hear from you in the meantime. It's only another couple of days, anyway."

"Yes, all right," Dave found himself agreeing, although he'd never once let a day go by without calling his father or Denise while he was on a trip. Never once. "That'll be fine."

"Okay, have fun, Davey!"

"You, too, mate," he replied with a pang of parting. And then they hung up, and Dave drove back to the camp where Nicholas waited for him – and even from such a distance away, Nicholas's long tall figure was clear and pale and warm in the last of the evening light.

After breakfast the next day, the two of them walked back down to the waterhole. Everything was exactly the same, of course, with the possible exception of the place being even more beautiful in the cool morning light.

Nicholas was too tactful to ask again about them moving the campsite down there; he simply went to check on his pupae. He took some more photos and made some notes, and eventually came back to join Dave by the side of the pool. The water was clear and inviting, but beyond the jewel–like green–blue surface it seemed fathomless. The Barcoo grunter ancestor had obviously gone *deep*.

"All right," said Dave eventually.

"Yes?"

"We'll pack up camp, and move down here."

"Thank you, David," was the quiet response. But Nicholas was grinning like a madman, Dave knew that even without looking at him. A very fond and enthusiastic and beautiful madman.

"This morning?" Dave asked.

"Yes, please."

Dave sighed, and finally turned towards the fellow. "All right, then. Let's get to it."

eight

It finally happened that afternoon. They'd set up camp, and then eaten lunch together. Nicholas had washed and dried the dishes, and then he'd headed off to wander around documenting the area surrounding the dark gold wattle. Dave spent an hour or so fussing around the campsite, making sure everything was organised as it should be.

Eventually, though, even Dave had to declare himself satisfied. He put a kettle of water on to heat on the gas stove, and ambled over towards Nicholas to ask whether he wanted a cup of tea, even though he already knew the answer would be yes. Maybe it was just an excuse to summon up another of those smiles. Dave pictured it now: the pleasure and happiness and gratitude lighting Nicholas up from the inside, his lovely lips curving and his dark blue eyes glowing … Dave was beginning to admit to himself that he was not immune to the charms of this man. Which didn't mean that anything need necessarily happen, of course, and actually no doubt nothing ever would, but still. It was kind of an earth–shattering thing for a straight Aussie bloke to deal with, when the only thing he'd dreamed about for all the years of his life was Denise and their own versions of little Zoe.

And that was when it finally happened. Dave was mulling over a few last poignancies for Denise and all the things that could never now be, and Nicholas was walking towards him with just exactly the pleased, happy, grateful smile Dave had imagined lighting him up – Nicholas was saying, "You're making tea? You wonderful man, you must have read my mind!"

When Dave suddenly froze. "Stop," he said quietly, lifting his hands just far enough to insist on stillness.

Nicholas froze, too, and for a moment he was wide–eyed with fear, trying to glance sideways at the waterhole without moving more than his eyes, perhaps thinking there must be a crocodile emerging to stalk them, or something equally dire. "What is it?" he whispered after a moment.

"Stay still," Dave advised. "I'm going to reach for your camera." It was tucked into the top of the open satchel at Nicholas's left hip.

By the time Dave straightened again with the camera in his hands, Nicholas had made a better guess, and was almost quivering with anticipation. "Is it … ?"

"A scrap of the sky. Yes. On your Akubra."

"Oh, David … *You* bought me this hat."

He puffed out a silent laugh. "I didn't realise it was a butterfly catcher, too." He took a pace round to his left, and slowly lifted the camera. Zoomed in, and focussed it. Took a few snaps with the butterfly filling the screen. Even while concentrating on photographing it, Dave was astonished by its beauty. A vibrant blue, with black markings, and scalloped curves round the edge of each wing, trailing down to long black tail–like things. Just amazing.

Dave zoomed the camera out a bit, and took a few of the butterfly and the Akubra, and Nicholas's eyes peeking at him from under the brim, wild with excitement and joy. And then Dave slowly handed over the camera, so that Nicholas could scroll through the images on the display.

"Oh, *David* …" Nicholas breathed in awe.

The man was shaking now, and the butterfly was starting to stir again. Well, Dave knew what he could offer to tempt the thing to stay. He carefully lifted fingertips towards it, assuming it could sense his sweat somehow, get the scent of it, or feel the coolness of available liquid.

"Don't hurt it," pleaded Nicholas. "Oh, *please* be careful …"

"I will," Dave promised huskily, trying not to laugh at the *Be gentle with me* undertones. Sure enough, the butterfly fluttered and lifted away from the Akubra – Dave drew in a sharp breath, forcing himself to wait for it to resettle rather than risk reaching for it – and then it landed again. On his fingers. That long probing thing unwound, and what with its light feet and its snuffling way of drinking from him – and what with the tension – Dave almost burst into giggles.

But he didn't. He carefully brought his hand down so that Nicholas could see it, and then he stood still while the butterfly drank and Nicholas gaped; the man murmuring things every now and then about the butterfly's beauty, and then muttering about the proboscis, antennae, the thorax and abdomen, and other things that Dave was clueless about – not to mention, "Those *wings*. Those magnificent *wings!*"

Dave laughed, he couldn't help it. He was so damned happy for Nicholas's sake. Nicholas flashed him a grin which was the visual equivalent of answering peals of laughter – and then Nicholas managed to take a photo or two from different angles, before at last the butterfly had drunk its fill, and it gently lifted, and flew a lazy random path around them, and then spiralled up into the dappled sunlight, before heading back towards the wattle.

Nicholas gasped as if wordless, and Dave just laughed some more, wonderful deep belly laughs. They'd done it! They'd found Nicholas's butterflies! Dave expected Nicholas to just turn and go running off after the thing, to watch it, to find where it landed. To *not* let it go.

But, no.

Instead Nicholas shared Dave's laughter for another moment, drawing close, and he lifted his hands, long pale fingers curving out like precious butterfly wings – and then he was cupping Dave's face, still looking awestruck, astonished, jubilant – he was cupping Dave's face, and leaning in close.

And then it happened.

They were in the midst of it before Dave formed another thought, and he could never afterwards say quite how it all came to be, but the truth was that they were kissing, they were each kissing the other, and even in the shock of it Dave knew it was as much his own impulse as it was Nicholas's idea. And those plump pink lips were just as delicious as he'd always known they must be, and Nicholas was masterful and generous and amazing, his waist slim and his shirt cool under Dave's palms.

And then too soon and not soon enough, Nicholas broke away, and grinned happily at Dave, *with* Dave, as if they shared the most awesome secret, the two of them. His cool hands still light upon Dave's skin, his fingertips dragging delightfully as he slowly pulled away. One last press of that wonderful mouth on Dave's, and then with another laugh Nicholas did at last turn to go stumbling off, skipping off after his butterfly, his happiness radiating from him, singing from him – and Dave stumbled after him, to help in all the business of photographing, recording, note–taking, as the giddiness calmed a little but never quite ebbed away, and even though they didn't quite touch again Dave was just *possessed*.

They hardly spoke that evening. Dave cooked dinner and cleaned up afterwards, while Nicholas spent hours poring over his field guide and writing up his scribbled notes.

"I'm convinced they're something no one's recorded before," Nicholas announced as it grew late. "If anyone's even seen them, they didn't realise what they were looking at."

"I'm glad," said Dave with simple sincerity.

"And they're so very beautiful! More than I could have ever hoped for."

Dave just smiled at him fondly. Words were redundant.

"We'll have to watch through a full life cycle, if we can."

"How long will that take?" Dave asked.

"I don't know, it varies so greatly."

Dave just nodded. And after reading and scribbling and thinking some more, Nicholas quietly wished him goodnight, and slipped away to his tent.

Which wasn't what Dave had expected. But a significant part of him was very relieved.

Another part of him was frustrated and yearning, and Dave was certainly honest enough to admit that as he lay awake that night. An hour or more slipped by as he lay on his back in the sleeping bag on the narrow camp bed, breathing, just breathing, and wishing even though he hardly knew what he was wishing for. He could hardly envisage anything beyond that kiss, and the possibility of more of those kisses, and Nicholas's long pale fingers finding him out – and his mind baulked at imagining any more than that, but he couldn't deny that he yearned, he was nothing but yearning and dread.

"David?"

He had the chance then to consider whether the yearning outweighed the dread, or if it was the other way round, for he could make out Nicholas's silhouette just beyond the canvas by the door of his tent. But he couldn't decide. He couldn't decide.

"David …"

Another whisper, fainter this time. Though the first had been a question, it had been authoritative, but the second utterance of his name allowed for doubt. And after a moment the shadow narrowed and rippled as if turning to go – and Dave's heart was hammering loud in his ears but he managed to say quite clearly, "Yes."

And then Nicholas was slipping inside the tent, striding towards him on those long legs, kneeling by the bed. Those hands cupping his face again, fingertips pushing in to massage the sensitive skin by his ears, and then

Nicholas's mouth on his, masterful and passionate and so damned sweet. Dave groaned into it, he couldn't help himself, he'd been so very hungry for so very long, he hadn't even realised how hungry he was – he groaned again, and then Nicholas's tongue was pushing into him, pushing in, and after a moment's resistance Dave surrendered, and the heat of it swamped him. His head pressed back heavy on the pillow, and he lifted his hands and *clung* to Nicholas's arms just below his broad shoulders, Dave just *clung*.

After a while one of Nicholas's hands started drifting down, the fingertips dragging down sensitive skin to resettle at his chest, a thumb–pad rubbing at one of his nipples through his shirt – and Dave moaned a protest at the spiky sensation, hardly knowing whether it tickled or provoked, but as Nicholas continued regardless, it became clearer that it was pleasure, that it was almost unbearable, but it was *good*. And just as he'd learned that lesson, the hand drifted further still, and this time Dave's moan was encouraging, and Nicholas chuckled into their kiss, their mad mouthing which hadn't broken even once – until now, as Nicholas pulled back to sit on his heels, and he murmured, "Take off your shirt. Don't worry, nothing more than that. Take off your shirt."

Dave found himself obeying, half disappointed and half reassured and wholly confused to find that Nicholas didn't follow suit. They were both in t–shirts and boxers – well, Dave was now in his boxers only, with the sleeping bag still covering his lower half. He lay back again, and waited for Nicholas's next move or next instruction.

"Good," said Nicholas, before leaning in to take up where he'd left off, kissing Dave, with one hand cupping his cheek and then sliding lower to run fingers and palm around the column of his throat, while the other hand crept lower and lower, slipping smoothly under the sleeping bag, smoother still under the waistband of his boxer shorts. And then too soon and an agonisingly long time later, that exploratory hand at last pressed a palm against him, fingertips pushing down to wriggle at his balls, and that palm just grazing flatly against him, a light caress that wasn't half enough even though that would have been all it took if only there were some friction there, some pressure. Dave groaned in need – Nicholas echoed him – and then the caress firmed, that hand encompassing more – and the kiss broke again, though Nicholas peppered kisses over Dave's face and throat, groaning as deeply as if he were the one being touched. And it was so odd and yet so perfect, that hand rubbing up and down, all of that hand mapping his cock and his balls, every slide so random and each touch so unexpected, so intense, though it was nothing like what Dave did for himself, nothing like at all, but infinitely better which should have been impossible. *How did you know?* Dave thought raggedly. *How do you KNOW?!*

Nicholas was shifting, kissing Dave's collarbones now and then lower still to mouth at his nipples and then gnaw at them just roughly enough, and none of this was anything like what Dave had had before, but even though it was strange, he knew it was good. He knew it was good.

"Please," Dave asked, one hand still gripping at Nicholas's arm and his fingers probably digging in a bit hard – the other hand holding firm to the camp bed as if he might fall off. *"Please."*

Nicholas groaned, and the pressure and crazy rhythm of that hand intensified, while Nicholas's other hand slipped away …

Dave waited expectantly, but then he sighed a protest as he realised that Nicholas had reached down to work at himself with his left hand in a mad echo of how he worked at Dave. "No!" Dave cried, shaking at the man's shoulder. "No."

Nicholas lifted his head, and stared at him imploringly, imperiously. "I *need* to."

"I know, but – properly. Both of us." He had no idea what, though. Dave wasn't quite sure whether he was game enough to touch Nicholas yet, and of course he didn't mean – "Not *properly* properly. But not on your own like that."

Nicholas nodded, and glanced about him wildly for a moment. Then he ordered, "Stay still." And he pushed back the rest of the sleeping bag, letting it slide off to the tent floor – pushed down Dave's boxers, exposing him for a long moment – gazed at him hungrily while Dave both revelled in it and died of embarrassment – until Nicholas remembered himself and his need, clambered clumsily on top of Dave. They were lying there together now, and Dave's arms were around the man – it was quite impossible on the narrow bed, of course, but Nicholas lifted up onto one side, just enough to slip his hand down between them, and –

And they came like that, only moments later, with Nicholas wrapping both their cocks up together in one long–fingered hand, tugging arhythmically, and leaning down to kiss Dave like a starving man – until the end, so soon, too soon, when Nicholas lifted his head again and cried out as if his world was ending, and Dave clung on and stayed with him the whole damned way through.

Dave lay there for a long while after, overwhelmed. Cradling this man in his arms, Nicholas, so strong and yet so fragile. So unexpected and yet so inevitable. Nicholas was a wrecked weight upon him, his face pushed close into Dave's throat, and they were warm, pressed too warm together, but God it was good, it was so fundamentally *good*.

Eventually Nicholas lifted his head, cast a discreet glance at Dave, but then kept his gaze averted as he clambered back off Dave and off the bed to crouch beside it. Then he had to gather himself to look at Dave more closely, and it was clear that Nicholas was nervous about what he might find. It was obvious that Nicholas was worried for his own sake as well as for Dave's.

The problem being that Nicholas was supposed to be the one who knew what the hell was going on. Dave felt a flash of fear and insecurity.

Which Nicholas must have seen, for a moment later, his long face cooled into something calmer. "Are you," he said, before clearing his throat and starting again. "Are you all right, David?"

"Yes," he managed in a whisper.

"That wasn't, er …" Nicholas glanced away for a moment, but then his gaze returned. "If I presumed too much –"

"No! No, it was great. You didn't."

"– forgive me."

There was nothing to forgive, of course. Dave reached to gently shake the man's shoulder. *Don't be an idiot.*

Nicholas stood, brisk now. "Let's get you cleaned up." He looked around, but Dave had a towel and face washer, bottled water and a washing bowl, just as Nicholas did in his own tent. Nicholas poured out some of the water, brought it and the face washer over to Dave, and cleaned off their mingled spunk, before setting his boxer shorts to rights again, and lifting the sleeping bag back over him. Then he took the bowl away, and quickly cleaned himself as well, keeping his back to Dave. Rinsed out the face washer, and leaned out the door to toss the water away.

Dave lay still, waiting. Eventually Nicholas returned. But he only leaned down for a moment to take one of Dave's hands and lift it, cradle it to his cheek with both of his own hands, press a kiss to the palm. And then he put Dave's hand back, and said quite formally, "Good night, David. Sleep well."

And he was gone.

Dave blinked, hardly knowing what to make of what had happened. But it had been good. It had been as close to inevitable as made no difference, he could see that now, and it had been good.

He turned over onto his side, facing towards where Nicholas's tent stood only a few metres away. And with a wistful sigh, Dave slipped away into peace.

Dave woke a bit later than usual the next morning. When he emerged from his tent, he discovered that Nicholas was already up and dressed, and sitting on a blanket on the Cruiser's bonnet, leaning back against the windscreen – though there was no point in trying to watch the sunrise while they were down here by the waterhole. The two of them greeted each other silently, with a nod and tentative smiles that soon broadened in response. Dave put the kettle on for tea, and went through his usual routine. Then he took the mugs of tea over to the Cruiser, and needing only the barest hint of an invitation he climbed up to sit beside Nicholas.

"I thought you'd be off with the butterflies," Dave said, tipping his head towards the wattle. They'd deliberately set up camp at as much of a distance as they could, so as not to disturb anything.

"They're not up yet."

"Late risers? Sensible creatures."

"But look at what they're missing," Nicholas said, a hand indicating their surroundings while his eyes lingered on Dave. "It's such a beautiful day …"

"It is," Dave agreed, and as they sipped the hot tea they contemplated the red rock and the green–blue jewel of the pool, the white–grey of the tree trunks reaching tall and the grey–green of the foliage. "It's *really* beautiful," Dave murmured, wondering if he just hadn't looked properly before, or whether all his senses were heightened, because –

"David –"

He turned towards Nicholas – and those long fingers were plucking the empty mug from his hands, Nicholas was reaching to stow their mugs on the edge of the roof rack behind him – and then Nicholas was taking Dave's face in his hands again, kissing him, *kissing* him, and they were making out – Dave was lying back, with Nicholas close beside him, Nicholas with those long legs curled under himself as he leaned in over Dave and *kissed* him.

Dave reached a hand up to grasp Nicholas's arm again, to anchor himself. The pleasure didn't inundate him as quickly this time, but that was all right. He still wanted this in the clear light of day, and he really didn't mind if they eased their way carefully into it. They kissed for long moments, for ever, and at last Dave let his hand slide down to find Nicholas's narrow waist again. He thought – Today, he thought, he could touch the man. Today, he was pretty sure, he could cope with that.

Nicholas murmured agreeably as he pulled away and sat up. Shucked off his shirt to reveal a pale chest with virile dark scatterings of hair, the man slim enough for his ribs to undulate down his sides, yet strong enough for those surprisingly hefty shoulders to impress.

"All right?" the man asked as he reached to start unbuttoning Dave's shirt.

"Yes."

The fingers stilled, as Nicholas apparently sensed a doubt. "David?"

"Let's … just take our time. If you can."

Nicholas looked at him drolly. "Haven't I already proved that I can control myself?"

"Yes. Mostly," Dave added with a grin.

"Well, then." Those long fingers continued, and Nicholas quirked a smile at Dave. "We'll take it slow, and I'll do what you tell me."

Dave was lying back, wallowing in being taken care of, having long since handed over control of all this. "I don't wanna tell you," he argued peaceably. "I just want you to – do stuff."

The smile turned wry and wonderful. "It will be my pleasure to – do stuff to you," Nicholas replied. "But then … along the way … you must tell me if there's anything you *don't* want. Will you promise me that?"

"Promise."

Nicholas helped Dave out of his shirt, then let him settle back before leaning in to press kisses across his chest, to suddenly rasp his tongue against a nipple. Dave's breath hissed, and Nicholas sinuously wound up to kiss him again. Against his mouth, Nicholas murmured, "Do you think we might get naked this time?"

"Reckon we could." So, it would be a first, but they were well past worrying about that, weren't they?

"My boy bits won't put you off?"

"Didn't seem to last night."

"But you didn't have to *look* at them …"

"Felt them, though. Against mine. No mistakin' 'em for anything else."

Nicholas chuckled filthily, and he sat up again, his fingers already working at his own jeans. "David, you are a constant revelation to me."

"Likewise, I'm sure."

"Oh …" Nicholas happily murmured.

And moments later Nicholas was straddling Dave's thighs, his hips shifting rhythmically as he rocked his cock hard along Dave's, both of their cocks wrapped up together again in one of Nicholas's beautiful hands – just like the night before, except this was daylight and they were naked and there was no question anymore about who they each were and what they each wanted. Dave's hands wandered boldly of their own accord, sliding up Nicholas's long thighs, feeling the muscle work below the cool skin, then shaping themselves to the man's sharp hip–bones, before finally easing around to fit up against the subtle curves of Nicholas's rear.

So different to what he was used to, and yet reassuringly the same in some ways, as Denise had liked to take a turn on top, and often she'd have him sit up against the pillows like this so she could lean in and kiss him when she wanted – just as Nicholas was doing now, swooping in to mouth at him hungrily – though Nicholas was undeniably different, and he seemed to have this habit of not just kissing but *caressing* Dave's face with his own, and it felt odd but amazing to have Nicholas's cheek slide along his own, the tip of Nicholas's nose gently rub across his closed eyelids, Nicholas's forehead roll against his, then those teeth carefully gnawing at the corner of his jaw before pushing lower to worry at his earlobe …

Dave had been without for too long to last – and he had too few defences against the surprises of a man loving him. In the end it wasn't any one particular thing that tipped him over the edge, but a combination of Nicholas curling in to bite at a nipple, and his own back arching deliciously in response, and Nicholas moaning his appreciation so that the sound vibrated through Dave's chest, and a stutter in Nicholas's rhythm followed by a twisting tug of their cocks – and Dave was shaking and shouting, and just *fountaining* out a week's worth of spunk – and Nicholas was laughing in joy – and the bastard waited, saw him through it all right to the last shudder, and didn't let up in the slightest, but kept going, rubbing his own cock against Dave's softening sensitivities which was just excruciatingly exquisitely wonderful – until Dave couldn't bear it anymore, and growled, grasping that narrow rear in his hands, hauling the man to him, insisting *"Now!"* – and Nicholas came with a howl right in Dave's ear which was both pleasure and punishment.

And when he was done, Nicholas fell back to lie against the Cruiser, but took Dave with him, so that Dave unexpectedly found himself curled against the man, holding and being held, in the utter comfort of completion.

He must have dozed off.

Dave came to a while later feeling a bit too cool, a bit too stiff in the thigh muscles, a bit too itchy where the sticky patches were drying on his stomach. "Ngh," he grumbled, shifting back a little, and reaching down to scratch.

"Stop!" came an urgent whisper – and Nicholas grasped Dave's wrist with iron strength.

"What … ?" he complained, even while he obediently stilled again. And then he felt a telltale tickle down amidst the wet spots. "Oh fuck …"

Nicholas chuckled – though he warned, "Don't you *dare* hurt it."

"As if." Dave had managed to open his eyes, and now peered down to find exactly what he'd feared. Nicholas's butterfly was drinking from his skin. And this time it wasn't sweat. "Fuck's sake!" he exclaimed, not knowing whether to be appalled or amused. "They're as queer as you!"

A happy guffaw met this declaration. "You are *so* lucky my camera isn't in reach."

"Oh God …"

"How could I resist? My three favourite things: cocks, balls, and butterflies."

Dave sank back, letting his head thud against the Cruiser. "That's four things."

"My four favourite things in all the world," Nicholas lightly confirmed. "Your cock … your balls … our butterfly …"

Dave laughed. He had to laugh, or he'd cry. "This is *way* too weird for me. You didn't tell me I'd be participating in butterfly porn!"

"Tit for tat," was the tart response. "You can't tell me this hasn't always been a fancy of yours … being debauched atop the Cruiser."

Some kind of *too much* sound bubbled out of him, and Dave stirred himself to flap a hand towards the butterfly – though not too close, so it probably wasn't any use. "Shoo!" he tried. "*Shoo!* Go on! There's a whole damned waterhole over there for you to drink from."

"Oh, but I'm sure you are so much sweeter," Nicholas murmured, curling up against him, and watching the butterfly but also snuggling his head in against Dave's shoulder. "I'm envious. I want to taste you."

"Not safe, I suppose," Dave said, after a moment's thought. The weird thing being that he hadn't ever had to worry about such things before. "Um …"

"It's all right, I realise you're probably a fine healthy specimen, and as far as I know I am, too, in that regard – but I won't do anything that isn't safe."

"Thanks."

Nicholas fervently burst out, "*God,* I want to get my mouth on you, though …"

"I want that, too," Dave had to admit. "It was your mouth … It was your mouth I noticed first."

"Yes … ?"

"Your smiles. I like the way you smile. And, um … your lips are pretty. No offence."

"None taken," Nicholas immediately replied. He tilted his head for a moment to frown up at Dave. "Do you really think I'd mind you finding my lips pretty … ?"

Dave had to grin, though he felt rather sheepish. "No, I don't suppose you would." They looked at each other for a long moment. And then Dave leaned in and pressed a kiss to those pretty lips, because that was only fair and right, and the contentment in Nicholas's smile afterwards was ample reward if any were needed.

Sweet still moments passed.

Until at last Dave couldn't bear it anymore. "I've got to move," he said. "Sorry to interrupt the feast and all that, but I want to clean up."

"It's all right. You've been very patient."

"If I just start shifting off the Cruiser …"

"I'm sure he'll get the idea and drag himself away. We know we have to let you go sometimes."

"Huh," said Dave, as he gingerly started sliding across to the side of the bonnet.

Nicholas was off the Cruiser and on his feet a moment later, his hands out to offer support if needed. "Could we have a dip in the pool? Did you test the water?"

"There's an idea!" Dave finally lowered himself to the ground, and at last with his dining table vertical the butterfly lifted off, and started fluttering around just over their heads. "Let's see if this one will come along, too. I think a change in diet is required."

A gurgling laugh from Nicholas, before one of his cool hands slid into Dave's. "Come on, then!"

"I don't want you drinking any of the water, mind," Dave lectured him as they walked down to the waterhole, both of them still bollocks–naked. "It seems safe, but there's no point in taking any risks we don't need to."

"Yes, David."

"And no diving in or anything. At least not until we explore a bit and make sure there's nothing hidden under the surface."

"No, David."

"Just a quiet dip, like you said."

"I might have to kiss you while we're in there, though," Nicholas said very seriously. "I'm giving you ample warning."

"Fair enough," said Dave quite stoically. And when Nicholas finally slipped into the jewel–like water to join him, Dave let the man gather him into his arms, and he suffered himself to be kissed.

nine

Nicholas had hardly said anything all morning, but it was perfectly obvious that something was going on with the butterflies. If the increase in activity hadn't clued Dave in – with photos being taken, notes being scribbled, and comments being muttered as Nicholas riffled back and forth through the field guide – then he could hardly be immune to the tenseness of suppressed excitement.

Still, the butterflies were Nicholas's concern, and Dave was happy enough pottering around the campsite, or sitting back with his feet up and *Clarissa Oakes* in hand, contemplating the sun gentled by leaves and pouring down softly on the water. The pool was as quiet as it had always been, though Dave had often thought to wonder whether there were actual Barcoo grunters in there. He found that he kind of hoped so.

Late morning, Dave took a mug of tea over to where Nicholas sat cross-legged by the wattle. "Here you are," he said.

"Thanks," Nicholas replied. He scratched his head through that thick thatch of dark hair, and belatedly tipped a sweetly distracted smile up at Dave. "Thank you."

"No worries." Dave let a beat go by before asking in a tone he was careful to make no more than mildly interested. "What's happening?"

"Well …"

Dave didn't push – but he noticed that Nicholas had been frowning over the manual for his video camera, not the field guide as Dave had assumed. "Um … Can I help with that, at least? Isn't it working, or are you just trying to figure out –"

Nicholas was nodding. "– whether it can do time–lapse photography, whether there's *any* kind of timer, or programmable thing …"

"Oh. I think that's gonna be a bit outside its specs." Dave sank to sit beside Nicholas, and took the manual when it was offered. "Why d'you need it? We're here now. If we set up the camera on its tripod, we can just take a shot ourselves every hour or whatever. We can work out a schedule, or –"

Dave ground to a halt.

Nicholas just looked at him, kind of both wide–eyed and glum at the same time.

"You want to set it up for tomorrow," Dave concluded, "when we're due to go into town."

"They're emerging," Nicholas whispered in hoarse intensity. "Some of the pupae are beginning to break open. The butterflies are starting to emerge from the chrysalis."

Dave nodded. He understood. God, he had it bad for this guy. "Obviously you'll have to stay."

It was perfectly plain that Nicholas wanted that more than almost anything. But he said, "I can't. I promised you –"

Dave gusted a sigh. "I think, under the circumstances, we can break that rule one more time."

"No, I don't want to take advantage –"

Dave just had to scoff at that. "Bit late to be worrying about that, mate!"

"Oh, David …"

"And how stupid was I?" he added rather disgustedly. "I thought you'd be wanting to have your way with me in a real bed!"

Nicholas became nothing but grin. "You'd share my bed in town? We'd share a room … ?"

"I should have known better. It's always the butterflies with you."

"David –"

"Well, all right. Maybe in a town where nobody knows me."

"*Is* there a town around here where no one knows you?"

"No."

"Oh."

Nicholas sounded so forlorn that David couldn't help chuckling. "Don't fret. I'm sure the discreet shared use of a double bed is somewhere in our future. Just not tomorrow night."

"Are you sure … ?" Nicholas actually seemed quite torn between the two prospects.

"Of course I'm sure. I can wait a week, and so can the bed. But it sounds like the butterflies can't. They wanna become fabulous, and they want it right now!"

At which Nicholas was just *glowing* at him …

"Um … But I'd better go in myself. Just for the day again. I promised Denise I'd call her, and she'll worry if I don't. I mean, we could get by for a while on the food we have, but I think I'd better go anyway. Denise will –"

"Yes," Nicholas said, cutting him off.

"I *do* understand, you know," Dave said, heading off down another path, which for some reason felt just as aggressive. "This is what it's all about for you, isn't it? The change from one thing to another. From a grub to something beautiful."

Silence.

Dave felt like an utter bastard. Though he couldn't have even explained to himself why. He let a few beats go by, and then started again in friendlier and more professional tones. "Is there anything you need? Anything you want me to do?"

"Send a Tweet," Nicholas replied readily enough, "to Charles and to Simon. Tell them … Nicholas has found his butterflies."

"I will."

"And then come back to me."

"Well, I'm *hardly* gonna leave you out here!"

Nicholas cast him an enigmatic look. But then he unwound and knelt tall beside Dave. Cupped Dave's face in both hands again, and bent his head to kiss him. His usual masterful style seemed undercut this time by a hint of wistfulness. "Come back to me," he murmured again, with his lips against Dave's.

Dave headed for Cunnamulla, and for once he was all business. He left the Cruiser at the mechanic's for a quick check–over and tune–up, dropped off their clothes at the laundromat, did the grocery shopping, ate a hamburger at the best of the takeaways while considering the other items on his list. Although the first thing he'd done, of course, had been to use his mobile to send the tweet as Nicholas had asked him.

Almost an hour later, he received his first response: *Takes a lot to make old charlie speechless. You found it didnt you?*

Yes we found it, Dave tweeted back, assuming Charlie meant the waterhole.

Come see me next week and tell me all. Both of you if he will come too.

Sure. I'm sure he'll be happy to. See you then!

And then in the late afternoon, just as Dave was getting into the Cruiser to drive back, the second response came through: *Excellent news to wake up to. Please give our congratulations and love to Nicholas. Thank you, Mr Taylor.*

To which he replied, *You're welcome, and I will pass that on. It will make him smile one of those big beaming smiles.*

It was only after he'd thumbed the Tweet button that he thought, *Too much!* But it was also too late. Dave quickly turned the phone off before he was forced to face just how easily he could be seen through.

The satnav gave up on him again, of course, but based on the distance he'd driven that morning Dave knew he was within five kilometres of the waterhole. He kept driving, quite confident that he recognised the landscape, that he was in the right place. He'd get there on instinct, he'd simply head straight there, no problems. They'd laugh about how easy it was to find after all. He'd crest that long rise and head back down again, turn left up the old creek bed, and he'd be back with Nicholas before the sun was even close to setting.

Except that rise never quite appeared, the road seemed level all the way to the distant horizon, and there was no sign of any dusty old water courses.

"Fuck," Dave eventually muttered, chewing at his bottom lip. He'd done almost ten kilometres now, which meant he had to have passed it. After another hopeful minute or two, he stopped the Cruiser, and got out to look around and see if he could get his bearings.

Nothing. He had a good sense of direction, but there was nothing to go on, nothing distinctive to see.

"Right." He got back in, and turned the Cruiser around. He was sure he hadn't gone wrong already, so he slowly retraced his trail, looking for the creek bed again, remembering how it had crossed the road. Once he'd done another ten kilometres, he stopped again, and tapped at the satnav, wondering if it would come back to life. It didn't.

His belly was this hollow stone sitting heavy within him, but he refused to give in to the dread. There was no point in being anything but calm and thoughtful. He had to find his way to Nicholas before it got dark, that was all. And he'd do it, too. If not, he was sure that Nicholas would be fine for a night, and so would Dave. He could sleep in the Cruiser. Nicholas would trek out to the rim of the wider valley the next morning to use the satellite phone, but he was perfectly capable of doing that, and by the time he'd returned to their camp Dave would have found him again anyway ...

Dave sighed. No, he had to get back that evening. He *wanted* to. He was desperate to. Nicholas would be fine, really. But Dave couldn't bear to risk it.

He wondered if he'd gone wrong somehow and ended up on a different track. Although he was sure they'd been heading west when they first found the valley, so perhaps this road ran parallel to the one they'd driven before. Which meant that from here he needed to turn left, and strike out across the countryside, hoping to come at the valley from the opposite direction.

It was a wrench. It took an actual physical effort to force himself to turn against his instincts, to deliberately head what felt like the wrong way. "Oh God," he muttered under his breath. "Maybe I have to *not* want to find him ..." It was impossible. His every instinct clamoured against such a notion. "Don't ask that of me."

There was nothing. For a long time, which was probably only a moment or two, there was nothing.

And then a bit of the sky moved, off to his right – almost exactly where he least expected it – and his heart tripped as he realised he was driving up across a slow rise.

"Thank you," he breathed.

He turned the Cruiser, and soon was looking down across the wide shallow valley, and there was the slightly denser foliage that hid their waterhole – a few bits of sky were dancing low over it in the last of the sun, and Nicholas was waiting for him. Nicholas was standing there where the track led down towards the waterhole, and his figure was tall and pale and fine and *glowed* in the sunshine.

Dave felt as if he'd found home.

But *hell*, he'd almost mislaid a client. He'd broken the rules, and he'd almost been badly caught out. And Nicholas – Oh God, Nicholas –

The thought wouldn't quite come, but what if the man had ...

Dave was a bit shaky by the time he got down there, and he was almost grateful for Nicholas's firm hand grasping his forearm as Dave climbed down from the Cruiser.

"Are you all right?" Nicholas asked, apparently concerned.

"I'm fine. Are you?"

"Yes, it's been a quiet day. A wonderful day. Thank you."

"Good."

Nicholas considered him for a long moment. "For once you look paler than me! Are you sure you're –"

Dave cut across him hoarsely. "I think I had to *not* want to find you."

"Oh."

"I couldn't do it. I couldn't do it. It was sheer bloody luck –"

"David," Nicholas said in hushed yet fervent tones.

"Don't ask me to leave you alone here again."

"I won't, I promise. *I won't.*"

"Yeah?" Dave asked, wondering if it would really be that easy.

"Yes. I'll come with you. I'll stay with you." That hand shook at his arm, and Nicholas gently scoffed, "Just try and be rid of me. See how far you get."

"I don't want –" he said brokenly. Unable to finish.

"It's all right," Nicholas whispered, "I know. David, I know …"

And Dave couldn't resist any longer. He hadn't wanted them falling into each other's arms and kissing passionately and all that nonsense. He hadn't wanted them to make anything more of this than what it was. But he'd gone long enough now without a kiss, he'd denied Nicholas long enough, so somehow he signalled that he was ready, that he wanted – and Nicholas, awake to every little nuance, kindly obliged.

They drove down to the waterhole, and Dave cast a glance around the camp to find that it was all, of course, in good order. He smiled at Nicholas as he turned off the ignition, and before they climbed out of the Cruiser he asked, "How are the butterflies?"

"They're fine. They're fabulous! There's a few of them emerged today."

"I saw some over the treetops."

"They'll be settling for the night now."

"Show me," Dave said. As he got out, one of the butterflies fluttered over and landed on his forearm. The thing just sat there; it didn't even start drinking from him. Dave tried not to disturb it as he walked around to meet Nicholas in front of the Cruiser.

Nicholas laughed. "It's your old friend! He's taken quite a fancy to you …"

Dave peered down at the thing. "How can you tell it's the same one? Does he have particular markings on his wings … ? Or is he bigger than the others? He was the first to emerge, wasn't he?"

More laughter, and Nicholas took his other hand as they walked towards the wattle. "No, I was just teasing. Or identifying, or something. Actually, butterflies don't get any larger once they're out of the chrysalis. They emerge full–grown."

"Oh."

"They were good ideas, though. I like the way you think. You should be a scientist, too."

Dave cast him a sardonic look.

"You have an enquiring mind," Nicholas explained with light sincerity.

Dave was saved from any need to respond to that by the simple fact that they'd arrived. He watched as Nicholas crouched and peered into the wattle. His own butterfly lifted up and flew about for a moment before disappearing somewhere in the midst of the dark gold blooms.

"There," Nicholas eventually said, indicating where Dave should look.

He bent down and leaned his head in close to Nicholas's. Stared hard – and saw nothing.

"It's difficult to find them, but that's the point. They don't want to be preyed on."

"They close their wings up flat, right?"

"Right! And the underside is quite a neutral shade, sort of a slightly bluish grey. Well, you've seen the colouring on our friend. Maybe if you try a different angle …"

He would have thought the wings were still large enough to show up easily, even when folded up tight, but apparently not. Eventually he thought he got a glimpse – of a butterfly or a shadow, or a butterfly that camouflaged itself as a shadow – and he reckoned that would have to do. The twilight was drawing in.

"I think maybe … maybe next time you can show me properly," Dave said.

"All right," Nicholas replied, with a delighted smile, as if Dave had just asked him out on a date or something.

"Let's get those groceries unpacked!"

Nicholas chuckled, apparently almost as happy with the practical aspects of their camp as he was with anything butterfly-related.

They worked together well. Once they had the food stored away, Nicholas offered to get dinner started. Dave was grateful for the offer, as he had other tasks he needed to do. He began by unpacking the goods on the Cruiser's roof rack and sorting them onto a tarpaulin. Then, some he stowed in the back of the Cruiser – the things that needed more protection, or simply the things that fit. The rest he began stacking away neatly in his tent. They had still been each retiring to his own tent at night, and Dave figured they'd both be grateful if they could still have space of their own. But he had other plans for their sleeping arrangements now. Once the tarpaulin was clear again, he began working on those plans.

Nicholas had been humming away quite contentedly to himself, but he finally came over when he realised what Dave's grand purpose had been. "Is that … ?" he asked, with a wicked glint in his eye.

"Yeah." An inflatable double mattress.

"For … ?" Nicholas warily pointed to the top of the Cruiser.

"Yeah." Dave quit pumping for a moment, and considered the man very seriously. "But only if you can promise me you won't fall off in the middle of the night."

Nicholas cast a searching glance over him from top to toe. "Well, that depends on how hard you try to buck me off, I suppose."

Dave snorted. "Let's assume that's not an issue. Are you gonna roll off the edge in your sleep?"

"No …" He sounded a bit doubtful, though. Which was honest of him, for Dave assumed that Nicholas wanted very much for them to share a bed.

"It might not be an issue, either," Dave reassured him. "You know how the sleeping bags unzip, so you can lay them out flat?"

"Yes." He'd already got it, and that glint had turned into the first smoulderings of a fire.

"You can put one on top of the other, and zip them together to make a big double bag."

"Then I'm only going to fall off the Cruiser if you do, because I'll be sleeping all night with my arms around you, and maybe my legs, too, so you'll take me with you if you go."

Dave resumed pumping, looking down and hoping the gathering twilight hid his face. Because he'd been missing that. He'd been missing that simple comfort so very much, for so very long. "It's going to be fine, then," he concluded when he could be sure of his voice.

"It's going to be *wonderful*," Nicholas countered, before heading back to finish preparing their dinner.

Dave had passed on the messages from Charlie and Simon as they sat at the campfire with their dinners, and Nicholas had been suitably delighted. But after that they fell silent, both contemplating yet another step they were about to take which felt trivial in some ways and madly significant in others. Dave supposed that anyone else might feel they were rushing things, but for him it felt so comfortable, so easy. Sinking back into a happiness and a belonging that he'd wondered if he'd ever find again.

It did occur to him that maybe he was fooling himself, and he reminded himself occasionally that he didn't really *know* Nicholas yet. Although, on the other hand, after twenty years of thinking that he had gotten to know Denise, she still managed to turn around and do the shockingly unimaginable. So there might be something to be said for going with the flow, and having a holiday fling with someone who certainly seemed decent enough to trust. With Nicholas, at least, Dave knew ahead of time that he was going to be left behind again. They'd have their three months, and then he'd take Nicholas back to Brisbane airport, watch him disappear through the security gates – maybe Nicholas would turn for one last poignant smile – and that would be that. But at least this time there was no pretence, no promises either spoken or implied …

Dave sighed, and put the rest of his dinner aside.

"Not hungry?" asked Nicholas.

"Not really. It was great, though. Thank you. I like your cooking," he offered quite genuinely.

Nicholas eyed him for a moment, as if doubting him. But when he finally spoke, it turned out he'd had something completely different on his mind. "Did you buy condoms today?"

"What?"

"Along with the double mattress. I was just wondering if you'd –"

"I heard you!" Dave took a moment, wondering why that had thrown him so. Finally he answered, "No, I didn't."

"Ah." Nicholas's gaze slid away, and then he turned his head as well, so that it was impossible to make out his expression.

So far they'd done very nicely without. Dave had been perfectly happy with all the myriad ways Nicholas used his hands and his own cock to bring Dave off, not to mention Nicholas lying over him, rubbing off against Dave's cock or his hip, and driving Dave quite wild with it. The simple pleasures could be profound pleasures, too. But then Nicholas had expressed the wish a few times to get his mouth on Dave, and who on earth was Dave to argue against such an idea – but even the preliminaries of Nicholas going down on him were starting to cross the line, from what Dave understood of safe sex.

Eventually Dave said into the silence, in uneasy tones, "Look. I have a couple of boxes of 'em here. If you want –"

If he hadn't already come to a halt, Nicholas's sudden glare would have stopped him in his tracks. "Oh, right," Nicholas sardonically responded. "So much for your non–fraternisation rule. I'm not your first exception at all, am I?"

"Yes, you are," Dave countered, a bit mystified. "They're not for me, they're for clients. I like to be prepared, is all. With anything they might need."

"Oh." Nicholas quickly sank again, looking sheepish. "Sorry."

Dave shook his head. *Don't be.* He was a bit disappointed, to tell the truth. He'd have thought Nicholas knew him well enough by now to have figured that out on his own.

"Look," said Nicholas after another long moment. "Really I was just asking to … sound you out. See what you're thinking … about what we can be doing."

"You'd know better than me." Dave shrugged. "Whatever. Anything. I'm in your hands."

"Really … ?" Nicholas seemed flabbergasted.

"Well, I trust you. You know … Just not – Not going the whole hog, yeah?"

"Yeah," Nicholas echoed faintly.

"Not yet, anyway," Dave found himself saying – at which even he sat up and raised his brow in surprise. "Um, or not *ever*," he mumbled, probably fooling Nicholas about as well as he fooled himself.

"David ..." Nicholas breathed.

"Yeah, mate?"

"David, I think we'd better get the washing–up done. As soon as possible."

"Sure," he amiably agreed, standing up and collecting his plate. "Could do with an early night," he added with a yawn.

"Me, too," Nicholas fervently agreed. "Oh yes. Me, too."

He felt both strange and safe, lying there atop the Cruiser, with nothing between his skin and the stars but the foliage above and then Nicholas shifting over him, Nicholas's mouth roaming all over, those plump pretty lips dragging kisses across him, those teeth nipping and gnawing, that tongue swathing any small hurts and then rasping across sensitivities – *all* over, making even the most mundane places sexy, until Dave's whole body was just *singing*, was just *thrumming* with need.

"Please," he said at last when he didn't think he could take any more – he didn't think he even *wanted* the pleasure continuing. And he never used the S word unless he had to, but he wasn't so proud that he wouldn't beg. "Please ..."

Nicholas lifted up from where he'd been grazing up the inside of Dave's thighs. Nicholas lifted to kneel up tall, and he looked down upon Dave a bit remotely, as if measuring him, as if assessing. As if Nicholas could keep doing this all night, he wasn't even properly started yet.

Dave lay there spread before him, heavy with heat, boneless with pleasure, shamelessly open. He hadn't known there was a nakedness that went far beyond being naked. He'd never quite lost himself like this. "Please, mate ..."

At last Nicholas nodded, as if what he saw was satisfactory. He reached for the condoms, and carefully, deftly rolled one down onto Dave's cock. Dave groaned as even the brief brushes of businesslike fingers threatened to undo him. But Nicholas said, "Not yet," so Dave tried to hold on, or at least tried not to strive for the end. He wasn't sure whether, if he relaxed and let things happen, it would simply then unfurl within him without any further provocation at all, or if that would postpone it beyond any kind of reason.

"Not yet," Nicholas said again, admonishing him this time, warning him – which was fair enough, for Nicholas bent down again, and then he was taking Dave's cockhead into his mouth, and gently suckling on it, and Dave was groaning and crying out some kind of gibberish that was mostly vowels, and he hoped Nicholas took that naked nonsensical noise as a fitting tribute to just how awesome a lover he was.

Just when Dave thought he couldn't bear it anymore if he couldn't *come*, damn it, Nicholas pulled away again. When Dave almost, well, *whimpered* a plea and lifted a heavy hand to reach up for him, Nicholas murmured, "Stay still. It's all right. Just wait a moment." And he seemed to be doing something with the lube that Dave had bought with the condoms, which sent Dave's thoughts spiralling off into fear and need and he had to chant to himself to make himself keep still, *I trust him, I trust him, I trust him.*

As Nicholas bent down over him again, he caressed one hand around Dave's waist, and then his forearm followed, sliding in underneath, forcing Dave to arch up the small of his back, and he whimpered again, there was no other word for it, and he had no pride left at all – he whimpered to feel the arch and the way his thighs opened for Nicholas, the way his cock and balls yearned towards the man –

And that mouth was on him again, suckling not as gently now – so gorgeous so gorgeous – that tongue doing clever swirly things – and it was all intended to distract him of course from Nicholas's other hand which was delving fingertips down down along that ridge behind his balls, and Dave was just *all* of him so sensitised that of course that felt good, too, so good, and he groaned in surrender, knowing what was happening to him, and not really even wanting to stop it. He groaned as those fingertips ran down further still, and were sliding across the most sensitive skin of all, each dipping in against the pressure, just the finger–pad, there was no question of more – but of course that's what he wanted, he wanted more. As one of those finger–pads returned to rub against him, Dave grunted an assent, an incitement, arching up further, and –

Nicholas intensified his efforts; Nicholas *hummed* around him. Dave cried out wildly – and suddenly he was coming, he was coming, and it was fucking *marvellous*, and that finger slid into him, it was just that easy, one of Nicholas's long pale fingers slid into him like that's where it belonged, and it felt odd but awesome, and the pleasure rolled through him again, heavy and intense, and a third time, and then at last he sank down again, babbling something grateful in the wake of it.

Gently, oh so very gently, Nicholas disengaged his finger, withdrew his arm from under Dave's back. Lifted up to deal with the condom. And then he folded back down again, crouched over Dave, his arms bracketing him, and his face pressed against Dave's soft and tender cock.

At last as the pleasure ebbed away and the world returned around him, the night air, the foliage, the stars – at last Dave sighed his poignant satisfaction.

Nicholas lifted his head, and grinned wickedly up at Dave. "Good, huh?" he said, knowing the answer.

"Yeah, wasn't bad," Dave agreed.

Nicholas chuckled – or, rather, gurgled in appreciation.

And Dave couldn't do it. He couldn't do the wry Aussie humour. He was going to have his citizenship revoked, but it had to be said: "It was so bloody good … It was fuckin' fantastic!"

"I'm glad," Nicholas said.

And the man still hadn't moved to take his own pleasure, but was instead letting Dave wallow in his … Well, fair was fair. Dave sighed again, satisfied, and resigned to the worst. "And you?" Dave prompted.

"Mmm …"

"Your turn now."

"Yes." Nicholas slowly lifted a little, and shifted up, sort of stalking up Dave on his hands and knees. Watching him with hunger and need and just a hint of cool remoteness.

"If you want –" Dave said. They both knew what he was offering.

"Hush," Nicholas said, admonishing him again. "There," he continued, shifting his weight over onto one side. "Put your legs together."

"Bit late for that," he joshed, even as he obeyed.

Nicholas rumbled an agreement, a laugh, but he was beginning to focus within himself now; he was beginning to lose himself, too. The man moved back over Dave, his legs straddling him – and then he lifted up for a moment, arranged himself – and pushed down, his cock sliding hard and hot between Dave's thighs.

They both groaned in reaction, and then Nicholas settled himself, lying close over Dave. He began a slow but unrelenting rhythm, working himself off, Dave's hands settling on the narrow curves of his rear, feeling them flex as Nicholas rocked and shifted up and back, up and back. And to be honest Dave was too raw for this now. Nicholas was pressed so close to him that Dave's cock and balls were rubbed up and down in an action mirroring Nicholas's – and he could see that would work so nicely if he were still up for it. Well, maybe next time. For now it was the kind of exquisite that was almost painful.

But he bore it, because he sensed Nicholas wouldn't take long at all, and anyway the man deserved something in return for his generosity and his self–restraint. He could be having Dave now, and they both knew it.

Instead he was groaning again as the end approached, and he was letting his head fall to gnaw at Dave's nipples, each in turn, and beyond his mess of dark hair, Dave could see his shoulders and back wrought up and tense – until at last with a guttural cry Nicholas came, and wet warmth spread between Dave's thighs, easing Nicholas's way.

"Good?" Dave asked in a whisper, long afterwards, with Nicholas still lying hot and heavy upon him.

"Oh, mate …" was the only faint reply.

ten

Dave thought he was in for a great comic episode the next afternoon.

Nicholas had spent the morning happily observing and recording the butterflies as more and more of them emerged from their cocoons, their wings folded and damp, but slowly drying and spreading out into magnificence. The creatures were such an awesome bright beautiful blue and such a rich velvety black that it almost felt impossible they were natural; it felt more as if they'd been created, and the designer had gone just a little bit over the top. Once they could move, they settled on the dark gold wattle blooms, and sipped away at the nectar. It was pretty awesome.

Dave spent most of the morning watching Nicholas, who seemed as if he were in his idea of heaven. The only times Dave managed to tear his gaze away were when he went to make tea, or Nicholas had a task that Dave could help with.

After lunch, Nicholas reappeared from his tent rather self–consciously carrying a butterfly net. The kind with the long pole and the white cone of netting that Dave had thought belonged in the past along with Enid Blyton books and safari suits.

"You're kidding me," Dave said.

"Um … no, I'm afraid not."

And Nicholas, after one last pink–cheeked glance, went off stalking his quarry. It was all very amusing watching this gawky gorgeous guy pit himself against the grace and guile of the butterflies. Dave got a good few chuckles out of that, despite Nicholas's increasingly pithy requests that he be quiet.

But eventually, with a swoop and a surprisingly efficient twist of his wrists, Nicholas caught one.

And that's when Dave finally realised what the man was doing. What the purpose of all this was.

Nicholas was very carefully placing the net over an open jar on the ground, and gently encouraging the butterfly down into it. When this was finally done, he screwed the lid on firmly, and lifted it to watch with a cool eye as the creature fluttered about for a while, settled onto the white cloth bunched at the bottom – and then rose in a panic that was all too brief.

The thing was dead.

It lay there with folded wings the colour of shadows, hiding the only beauty it was left with. Nicholas reached in with those long pale fingers, picked it up by the body, and transferred it into a semi–transparent envelope. He was gentle now, but there was no pity in him. No regret.

Dave watched, kind of horrified. Though he couldn't really work out why. He'd known this would be part of the deal, even if he hadn't really thought about it. He'd known that Nicholas, during all those long days back in Brisbane, must have been examining hundreds of such specimens. And Dave wasn't a hypocrite. He ate meat, and loved it. He'd killed fish and animals – not many, but enough – and prepared, cooked and eaten them. He waged a perennial war on the pests that threatened to invade his home back in Brisbane. And yet there was something about this …

Maybe it was the simple contrast. Not so long ago, Nicholas had been standing amidst a storm of butterflies, his arms out in welcome, in celebration, in love – and his happy smile just *beaming* like it could light up the whole world. Like a sexy St Francis, in a black shirt and blue jeans. And now he was systematically killing them.

Not all of them, of course. Probably only a handful of samples, for himself, for the museum and university in Brisbane, and perhaps for somewhere equivalent back in England.

Nicholas shot him a defensive glare as he came back with another one in his net. *"Death comes equally to us all,"* he muttered.

It sounded like a quote – but whether it was or not, Dave could find no reply.

His own reactions puzzled him, but it made some things clearer still. Dave actually had to make an effort to give himself over to Nicholas's seeking hands that night. He really had to push himself past a wayward sense of reluctance. It was ridiculous. And yet that's what made it clear to him what was happening here.

He was giving himself over to Nicholas, he was letting the other man take charge. And he'd been happy to let Denise take the lead in all kinds of ways, but he'd seen that as equality and fair's fair. This … this was something more.

This was trusting someone else enough that he didn't need to be Dave anymore; he didn't even need to be one half of Denny–and–Davey. Instead, he became nothing that didn't belong to Nicholas Goring – even if it was only within these very limited circumstances, within this sleeping bag for an hour or two and no more. And he got such a fucking *charge* from it.

Nicholas began his attempt to win Dave over with gentle kisses, just pressing those lips against Dave's mouth and cheeks and forehead and chin with no expectation of response. His penitent hands stroked Dave's hair, and then his throat. Nicholas lay close against him, overlapping him, one leg bent so that Nicholas's thigh angled across both of Dave's, holding him there. And it didn't take much to keep him there, accepting these soothing caresses, even at the beginning. By the time Nicholas's free hand had stroked its way down to rest over Dave's heart as if feeling the beat of it against his palm – well, by then Dave had surrendered, and he was Nicholas's again.

"I won't hurt you," Nicholas whispered, when it was clear that he could have his way again.

"Yeah, you will," Dave responded evenly, "but I don't care."

And Nicholas bent his head to claim Dave's mouth in a full–blooded kiss, and gathered him up close in his arms. A hand began slowly caressing down his backbone, languorously pursuing its goal, knowing it wouldn't be denied.

Later, much later, Dave was finally allowed to come, held pressed close to Nicholas with his hips rocking helplessly between sensations, both of them otherwise still, and Nicholas murmuring, "That's it … Yes, that's it …" Rocking between the rough graze of his sensitive cock against virile dark hair and the rub of Nicholas's spent cock, the roll of his balls against Dave's thigh – and one of those long pale fingers deep inside him, not moving, but only letting him feel the slide of it as he rocked up and back, up and back. It was like nothing he'd ever imagined for himself, but Dave didn't mind the possession. Already, it felt sweet.

It was astonishing how many hours in the day Nicholas could devote to his butterflies: watching them, recording them, writing up his notes longhand in a journal. Nicholas had initially planned to type up his notes on his laptop, but of course that required power – and while they would put the generator on for a short while when necessary, it created too ugly a noise for their haven. While Nicholas was so happily engaged, Dave tended to the camp, and cooked for them both, or spent an hour or two reading. And the rest of the time – especially once twilight fell, and the butterflies settled for the night – was theirs to share.

"Pleasure can be learned," Nicholas asserted once, before rasping his tongue across a place it had no business being, following this with soothing little licks that tickled at first. When Dave laughed, and tried to squirm away, Nicholas had hushed him, and firmed his hold on Dave's hips. "Be still, relax. Pay attention. *Learn* this."

"Nicholas –" he protested. "You can't –"

But the man just bent his head and continued, and eventually the tickles became uneasy shivers and then provocative shudders, before at last it became too much, this sensation whatever it was, it was too much, and he groaned distraught and Nicholas took pity on him, wrapping palm and long pale fingers around Dave's cock, knowing just how to bring him off now, all the while lapping at him, lapping at him, until Dave shook to an exhausted halt, his nipples hard and all his nethers tender.

One afternoon, Dave saw that Nicholas was watching something particularly intently, and filming it with his video camera. Whatever it was was on the ground, and continued for a while. At least long enough for Dave's interest to be piqued, and for him to wander over there.

"*Don't* say anything inappropriate," Nicholas advised. "I'm filming this for posterity."

Two of the butterflies were flat on the ground with their wings spread, overlapping each other but facing in opposite directions. There was much fluttering and bumping about, almost as if they were trying to take off in this unlikely configuration. "What are they doing?" Dave asked – and he realised the truth even as he suggested rather pathetically, "Wrestling?"

Nicholas chortled, and replied in hallowed tones, "They're mating!"

Dave had to laugh. "There you go again with your butterfly porn."

"Yes. It's a beautiful thing."

"I'm sure it is." Dave considered the logistics. "Their tails … ?" It was all going on underneath the spread wings, but he couldn't think how else it would work.

"Yes. Their genitalia are in the last few segments of their abdomens –

what you think of as their tails. And they … engage back to back."

Soon it was over, and after … disengaging, the butterflies gathered themselves, and eventually flew lazily off back to the wattle. Nicholas followed them with his camera, but once they'd settled he turned it off and came back to where Dave still stood.

"Well," said Dave.

Nicholas was favouring him with a lascivious grin. Dave never had been able to resist that one.

In between, there was time enough to talk. They'd while away hours around the campfire, or sitting on the Cruiser's bonnet, or lying atop the roof watching the stars wheel about the sky. If they were close together, then Nicholas almost invariably had his arms around Dave, or at least a hand resting upon him, as if he just couldn't get enough.

"It's just as well you have a thing for the hired help," Dave commented at some stage. "An earl would hardly deign to notice me otherwise."

"I'm not an earl," Nicholas argued, "and what do you mean? You're a friend, not the help."

Dave felt a smile bloom in response to that, but he kept it to himself. "Your first was the chauffeur, your latest is me … Like a bit of working–class rough, do ya?"

"Idiot," Nicholas said, kissing and nibbling at the tender skin just beyond Dave's ear. They were curled up together on the Cruiser's bonnet and windscreen, and the night air was soft upon them. "I have a thing for gorgeous hunky men. Can't blame a fellow for that."

"Of course not, sir. You just have your way with me, sir, and then discard me, that's all right."

"Oh shut up!" Nicholas cried with a laugh. "I thought you Australians didn't believe in class."

Dave shrugged a little. "Not as much, maybe. It's a pretty egalitarian place. There's still rich and poor, though."

Nicholas finally sat back a little – not far enough to let go of Dave, but to consider him. "Why do you even care? I'm *not* an earl, and never will be. I'm the youngest son of an earl. Which hardly means anything at all."

"It means you've got the money to come over here for three months chasing butterflies.”

That earned him a scoffing laugh. “The family’s money came from my grandmother: a commoner in the grocery business. Our fortunes had sunk pretty low before she came along.”

“She’s a grocer?”

“Well. In a rather large way.”

“Oh.” Dave reflected on that for a while, and Nicholas returned to nuzzling him. There was so much he didn’t know about Nicholas, and probably half the things he thought he knew were wrong. Dave turned away a little and settled in more comfortably, hoping for a long story. “Tell me about your chauffeur,” he prompted.

“Mmm … Don’t know that there’s much more to say.”

“Did you and he … you know … do stuff?”

“Oh yes,” was the ironic response. “It was *that* romantic.”

“Come on … What aren’t you telling me?”

Nicholas sighed, and settled in behind Dave, his mouth against Dave’s nape. “I’ve kept the secret all these years. Why should I tell you? The man’s still associated with our family. And he married later; he has a family of his own. I’m not going to embarrass him now.”

“So, you did, huh?”

“Idiot … Well, don’t let your imagination run away with you. There might have been a kiss or two. It all seems so innocent now. So harmless. But it felt delightfully wicked at the time. And I really wouldn’t want to embarrass him, David. He was only being kind, and maybe he’s forgotten all about it. This has to stay between us, all right? Please.”

“Of course,” he stoutly agreed.

Then Nicholas asked, “So … tell me about Denise, then. When did that start?”

Dave huffed a laugh. “The very first day of school. I was five years old. Totally out of my depth. And she took pity on me. Took my hand, and led me about all day. She made me … She made me smile when all I wanted to do was cry. She was brave enough to face dragons, you know?”

Nicholas was still and hushed. Though when he finally spoke, it was only to lightly say, “Do you even have dragons in Australia?”

“Bunyips,” Dave insisted. “She’d have faced a bedevilment of bunyips for me.”

And Nicholas quietly commented, "You really have been in love with her your whole life."

"Yeah, it was just … Well, I never questioned it. She was always there. I assumed that … when she was ready to get married, she'd ask me. Or – not married. I figured that when she was ready to have kids and do that whole shebang, she'd let me know." He thought about that for a moment, and then added, "Which she did, I guess. Except it wasn't gonna be with me."

Nicholas's arms tightened around him, and they wriggled in a bit closer still until the fit between them was perfect. The stars wheeled overhead until at last the sense of loss was overtaken by the sense of belonging.

"David," Nicholas whispered, with his lips and his breath damp and warm against Dave's skin.

"Mmm?"

"Will you let me …"

"What?" he asked mildly, though he figured he knew. Of course this was where they'd been heading all this time.

"Will you let me fuck you? I want to – so badly."

He guffawed under his breath. "Not if you're gonna do it badly, no."

"Don't tease. I want to have you. I'm pretty sure you want that, too."

He let the minutes drift past. Eventually he said, "I'm game to try, all right? But not out here."

"I'll be careful," Nicholas assured him. "And anyway, it won't hurt as much as you think it will."

"No, well … that's not what I'm worried about. Or only a bit."

"*What*, then? I mean, why not out here?"

"Because –"

"Where better? This is *our* place. We're safe here."

"But if something goes wrong –"

Nicholas shifted up on an elbow so he could look at him properly. "Like what?"

"I don't know."

"*I* do. I know what I'm doing, David."

"I'm sure you do!" He wondered how many lovers Nicholas had had over the years. Obviously they would outnumber Dave's tally by *far*. None of which was the point.

"What's the point, then?"

"I just – Look. I don't have a backup plan for this one."

And apparently this made sense to Nicholas, or at least he was used to Dave by now, and all the care he took about their travelling, their camps, their safety. The fail–safes and backups and redundancies.

"All right," Nicholas agreed, leaning in to press a kiss to Dave's temple. "Next time we're in town?" he asked hopefully.

"Yes," said Dave. "Next time we're in town. We'll go to Charleville. We'll get a proper bed for the night."

Nicholas sighed with satisfaction. And for now they made do happily enough with bold hands and mouthy kisses.

eleven

They reached Charleville early in the afternoon. And their first task, Nicholas insisted, was to secure a room for the night. Or, more to the point, a bed.

Dave refused to be a coward about this, but oh God he really had to screw his courage to the sticking place. He fronted up at his usual hotel. Marge was at the reception desk, for which he didn't know whether to be thankful or not.

"G'day, Dave," she greeted him in her usual laid–back friendly tones. "Hello, love," she added to Nicholas who was quite naturally there at Dave's side.

"G'day, Marge," Dave responded, and Nicholas said, "Hello."

"Two singles?" she asked, though it wasn't really a question. She was already scanning down that night's register, and had picked out the rooms before Dave managed to force out a reply.

"Actually. One double, thanks, Marge."

She looked up with a carefully schooled face that didn't quite manage to hide her surprise. A glance flickered over both of them, before she evenly replied, "Of course." And she bent her head to run a finger down the register again.

Dave felt like dying would probably be an easier option than dealing with this embarrassment. But to be fair to Marge, she was probably more surprised that Dave the one–woman man was interested in anyone other than Denise; that Dave the scrupulously professional guide was sleeping with a client. She probably didn't really give a toss about Dave suddenly deciding he batted for the other team. She might actually, Dave told himself, find it hardest to forgive him for taking up with a Pom.

"Here we are, love," Marge eventually said, handing a key over, and taking the opportunity to pat Dave's forearm with kind reassurance. "Twenty–three on the first floor. It's an en suite. Usual rates for you, Dave, but it's our best room."

Right. Well, if his face hadn't been as red as a waratah before, it certainly was now. "Thanks," he managed to say – or squeak. He cleared his throat, and managed a rather more manly, "Thanks, Marge."

Nicholas smoothly added, "Thank you very much."

And there was no way in hell Dave was heading up there now, even if it *was* only to unpack. He turned to Nicholas. "Pub."

"Excellent idea," Nicholas agreed. "We'll see you later, Marge."

"See you, boys!"

And they headed off out the door, shoulder to shoulder, and Dave said, "Oh God, I am just going to *die*."

Charlie didn't even need telling. He was already sitting there, on his own at the same table as last time, as if waiting for them. He took one look at Dave and Nicholas as they walked towards him, his gaze encompassing *all* of them, and he *knew*, damn it. He knew they were together. In response, bless him, Charlie grinned like a particularly happy loon.

They had barely sat down when, in this pub with emphatically *no* table service, Rosie brought over three Cascades. "Here you are," she said, setting them down – and she *winked* at Dave. "On the house, boys."

The other two said their thanks very nicely, while Dave sank down further in his chair and just withered. God. It must be written all over him. *This man is in sexual thraldom to a queer English earling.*

He wondered how long it would take for the news to spread from the hotel and the pub on outwards. He was gonna be losing the very last shreds of his tattered virginity that night, and the whole damned town was gonna know exactly what was going on. *Dave Taylor is taking it up the arse … and loving it!*

Really. Dying would be so very much easier.

"You two have had a busy couple of weeks," Charlie eventually observed.

Nicholas laughed. "We have," he agreed quite happily. "The butterflies, Charles: they're so beautiful! More than I could have ever hoped for. Last week I got to watch them emerge, watch their wings drying out and spreading – and then flying for the first time! Well," he added with a chuckle, "that's never going to get old, but with these particular beauties …"

"And you're the first white fella to find them?"

"I think so, yes. Or the first to really identify them, anyway. There's nothing quite like them in the CSIRO field guide." Nicholas was looking pleased and proud, but he attempted to turn the conversation. "All that's for later, though. For now it's just a privilege to have all this time to spend with them."

Charlie persisted. "What white fella name you gonna give them?"

Nicholas's cheekbones turned pink, and he turned towards Charlie, shielding his mouth as if telling him a secret – but Dave was certainly meant to hear his loud whisper. "Actually, I think I'll name them after David." At which Dave went waratah red again. "But don't tell him! I'm mortifying him enough already."

That drew a rumbling chuckle from Charlie, who considered Dave for long excruciating minutes. But eventually all Charlie said was, "So, you found old man grunter's waterhole."

"Yes," Dave replied, feeling the ground a little firmer under his feet. "It's an odd place. But there's no sign of any fish there, so I don't know if it's really –"

"Yeah, you found it all right."

"There's nothing there but the butterflies. It's beautiful, but there's no birds or animals, no fish, no insects. Just the butterflies. Isn't that kind of weird?"

Charlie shrugged. "How does it feel to you?"

Dave sighed, and looked away.

"He feels like it *should* feel wrong," Nicholas supplied. "But it doesn't."

"Of course it doesn't," Charlie stoutly agreed. "You don't go drinking the water, though. You know that much?"

"Yeah, we know," Dave agreed. "We swam a couple of times, but we were careful." And now he thought about it, they had instinctively avoided bathing very much, when really he'd have expected them to be taking a dip every afternoon in that gorgeous jewel–like water.

Charlie nodded. "There's a mystery, a strangeness. My compass didn't like the place. It kept pointing me away."

"The satnav doesn't like it, either."

"Minerals," they concluded. "Heavy–duty mineral deposits."

Nicholas contemplated this. "Would that keep the birds and animals away from the water? But the butterflies have managed to adapt somehow?"

Charlie nodded. "Could be … Could be."

After a moment, when it seemed that they'd said all that could be said about that, Nicholas nudged Charlie with a friendly elbow. "If I have

Butterfly Dreaming, what kind of Dreaming does David have?"

And Charlie considered Dave again for long long moments. "I don't know, Nicholas," he eventually said. "I look at him now, and all I see is you."

Nicholas squirmed in pink–faced delight, giggling like he was still in high school, while Dave muttered, "Yeah, yeah. You always know just what to say, don't you, mate?"

"I always do," Charlie complacently agreed.

A while later, Dave decided that if Charlie knew, then it was only fair to tell Denise as well. And she would be expecting him to call anyway, in line with their new routine. He took the three empty glasses back to the bar, and speed–dialled Denise's number while he was waiting. Rosie was wise enough to leave him be for the moment.

The first thing Denise said when she picked up the call was, "Davey! I missed you!"

Even now his heart skipped a beat to hear her greet him so. "Yes. I'm used to talking with you every day. I missed it, too."

"How's the trip going? Are you all right?"

"Yes, everything's fine. Denise –"

"Are you still camped at the waterhole?"

"Yes. Look," he said. And he sighed. She knew enough to wait now, when in many ways he would have preferred her to insist on doing all the talking. He was sure she would have gotten to the truth in the end. "Look. Denny … I'm, uh –" he wasn't sure what verb to use, so he left the word incoherent. "I'm *nnngh* … with Nicholas."

A moment of silence. Then she burst out, *"Seriously?"*

"Yeah."

Another beat resounded before, "Oh, Davey, that's *marvellous*."

"Um. Really?"

"Yes. Yes, of *course*. God, I've hated that you've been alone all this time."

He laughed a little, under his breath. *Well, whose fault was that?* he thought. But all the heat of it had gone. All the bitterness had left him.

"Davey, I'm so happy for you."

"It's not too weird?"

"No, of course not. Love is love, wherever you find it."

"Oh. Uh, no one's using words like that, Denny."

She laughed. "Then a fling is a fling is a damned fine thing, Davey. Enjoy yourself, and I'll hear from you in a week's time, all right?"

"All right." And once she'd ended the call, he murmured, *"Goodbye."*

"You right, Dave?" Rosie asked, once she'd finally worked her way down the bar.

Dave smiled at her. "Three Cascades, thanks, mate."

The three of them spent quite some time poring over various maps, but they were really no closer to pinpointing the waterhole, or working out whose land it was on. There was a large Aboriginal reserve in the area, and the edges of two different privately held properties. But where the waterhole sat in relation to these seemed almost impossible to fathom.

"It's almost as if," Dave said, feeling idiotic but saying it anyway – "as if it's in–between."

"It's in the interstices," Nicholas said, as if he were agreeing.

Charlie just contemplated them both for a while, and then drifted off in thought.

After scratching their heads over the maps for a while longer, Nicholas and Dave left him to it.

Pretty much as soon as it was decently dark, Dave and Nicholas snuck up to their room with their overnight bags, managing to avoid Marge's notice – though Dave suspected that was more due to her tact than their own cunning.

Then it was just the two of them, which felt so familiar these days, it felt so safe. Nicholas wandered into the room while Dave locked the door. They put down their bags, but neither of them turned on the light – which was hardly needed, as there was a street light nearby pouring a block of cool light in through the net curtains. It was certainly enough to help them see what they were doing.

Nicholas must have realised that something needed sorting out, for he didn't kiss Dave or even touch him, but simply heeled off his shoes and sat on the bed, his back against the pillows and the iron railings of the bed head, and his legs stretched out long. And he waited patiently with his hands held loosely together in his lap.

Dave picked up the straight–backed chair and turned it around so he could sit facing the man, and then he thought about what he needed to say and how to say it. But in the end, of course, he just blurted it out. "Does everyone know what we're doing tonight?"

"Well, it seems that most of them have the general idea by now."

"I mean you fucking me. Is it really obvious? It feels like it's really obvious."

Nicholas took a moment with that, as if determined not to let this faze him – or not to freak Dave out by showing that it fazed him. "I would have thought," Nicholas eventually said, "if they *are* speculating about the details, they'll assume it's the other way round."

"Really?"

"Yes, what with me being gay and you being otherwise straight. I think that tends to be the assumption."

"Oh."

Nicholas let a silence drift by, before asking, "What bothers you: the fact that that's what we had planned, or the idea that everyone knows about it?"

Of course it was the latter, but Dave was too ashamed of his lack of courage to say so.

"I don't care what we do, David," Nicholas said, sincerely but also a bit coolly. "You can fuck me, if you'd prefer. I really don't mind."

"Yeah?" Dave had hardly even thought about doing that, but now that he considered it, he reckoned he could.

"Of course. We can save the rest for some other time. Or we can just do the things we've already done. Then again, we don't actually have to do anything at all." Finally he added, a bit more warmly, "David, I'll do anything you want."

The problem was, however, that Dave wanted to be fucked. He sighed. "How did you know? That this is what I'd end up wanting. Is it that obvious?"

"Not at all."

"I feel like it's … blazoned across my forehead, or something. In neon lights."

Nicholas settled in a bit, and began comfortably telling his side of the story. "When I first saw you, I assumed it would all be the other way round. I like to be in charge when it comes to sex. Doesn't say a lot about me as a person, but in bed, that's what works best for me. When I saw you … You're gorgeous, David. I don't think you realise how bloody gorgeous you are. I fancied you like nothing else. And you were this tough strong Aussie hunk of a man. And that first morning!" Nicholas laughed at the memories. "You were so efficient, so in control. You were laying down the rules, telling me how things would be, and I was following you around like a smitten little puppy with my tongue hanging out. I thought, well, nothing's going to happen, because you're straight, but if it ever did … then you'd be the one in charge. And I thought, that's how it must be when you holiday Down Under, everything goes topsy–turvy."

"So when did you realise?"

"It took me a while. I'm not usually that slow, or I hope not, anyway. I realised that a lot of the efficiency was about you being the best tour guide you could be, about you knowing the dangers, and making sure that no one in your care ever got hurt. There was another David underneath that, a more private man, who was happier to just go with the flow. There were times I felt as if you were … waiting for me. Then I'd tell myself that was just wishful thinking. It was only when we began …" He paused. Apparently Nicholas wasn't sure of the right verb either. "It was only when I kissed you properly for the first time that I started feeling the lure of you … the tug of you … inviting me in."

Dave let out a breath that definitely *wasn't* a gasp. But it was as if those last phrases were poetry, they were so true. Dave himself could feel the draw of the notion … of lying back and inviting Nicholas in. Not just in the obvious ways. And in that moment, he knew that it was going to happen that night – even if all of Charleville did know it, too.

"Nicholas," he said a bit brokenly, standing and letting his sense of direction guide him. His knees bumped into the side of the mattress.

And Nicholas was shifting towards him, his arms wide in welcome, and those pretty lips pursing for kisses and smiling in delight as he murmured, "My beautiful man …"

Dave had never had pretensions to poetry. As he turned within those strong affectionate trustworthy arms, letting gravity take him back down onto the bed, he said, "Fuck me. Nicholas, I want you to fuck me."

"Oh, I will, my darling David. I will – but all in good time."

"Close – getting close now – hurry up, for God's sake –"

"Mmm," Nicholas agreeably remarked, not stopping what he was doing, and not easing off or intensifying it, either.

"God's sake – *fuck me* – gonna go off any *minute* now –"

Nicholas removed his mouth from Dave's condom–covered cock for long enough to say in friendly tones, "As you wish. In your own time."

"*No!* No," Dave insisted.

Nicholas gurgled a delightful laugh around Dave's cock, and lifted his head again to hush him. "Stick to *yes, yes*, would you? Unless you *want* half of Charleville dashing in here to protect what remains of your virtue."

Dave groaned in frustration, having lost the sweet fine edge he'd been balancing on. Maybe that was just as well, though. This way they could take it careful and he could really concentrate on it. Dave lifted his head to stare at Nicholas, who'd inexplicably remained exactly where he was: between Dave's thighs, which was great, but penetrating him with nothing more than a long narrow finger.

"What the hell are you waiting for?" Dave demanded. "I'm good to go here! Fuck me already!"

"Not the plan."

He almost spluttered in indignation. How on earth could Nicholas get this so very wrong? "No. Obviously. I wanna come while you're –"

Nicholas was shaking his head. "Not the first time," he advised.

"Not – ?!"

"I need you relaxed for that. Post–orgasmic works just fine."

Was this really not clear? "No – No, I want to come while –"

"Coming involves tension," Nicholas argued implacably. "Which is not conducive to enjoying your first thorough rogering."

Dave glared at him and sank back, thoroughly disgruntled. And hard. Thoroughly disgruntled and ball–achingly hard. "Fuck's sake," he muttered.

"Enjoy this, you gorgeous thing, and then I promise you'll have a fair chance of enjoying the rest."

"But I wanna …"

"Next time. If you're up for it, having survived the first time, then next time we'll try for the whole nine yards."

Dave wanted to sulk for a while, but how could he when the oh–so–reasonable Nicholas set himself up so very perfectly? "Oh, now you're just trying to show off," Dave complained, "when I know very well it's not even nine inches."

Nicholas stared at him blankly for a long moment – before finally twigging, and the two of them burst into giggles. Not for long, of course, but it was enough for them to regain their equilibrium.

The mood had kind of ebbed away, so Nicholas – leaving his finger in place – shifted up far enough on an elbow and knees to lean in and kiss Dave – to mouth at him hungrily, to bite at his lower lip and suck it in and chew on it – and then to press his tongue into Dave's mouth, stiffly miming his ultimate intentions, echoing the slow relentless rhythm his finger maintained. Dave groaned around the luscious intrusion, and then tried chasing after when that bold tongue eventually withdrew.

"All right, my darling man?" Nicholas whispered with his lips brushing against Dave's – and Dave didn't want to lose that, he loved the intimacy of being in each other's faces when they came – so he answered by nibbling in turn on Nicholas's pouty lips, and reaching down a hand to shuck the condom and bring himself off. Which took hardly any time at all, with Nicholas lying over him, connecting randomly skin–to–skin as well as that mouth and that finger, and his pithily crooning encouragement …

Glorious.

And then – at last, before the glory faded – Nicholas got down to work, and for a little while Dave took himself away. He wasn't afraid anymore, he didn't think it would hurt, he wasn't even embarrassed now, but he figured he needed a time-out to see it through, to let it happen.

Which was probably completely unnecessary because of course Nicholas knew just what he was doing, and he'd prepared Dave so thoroughly … Far sooner than Dave had anticipated, in barely a few moments, Dave was surfacing again, eager for the full experience.

He was breathless with it. He was breathless, he was full of Nicholas, there was no room for breath in him. He was breathless, he was curled up below Nicholas on the bed, on his back with Nicholas over him, within him. His right hand clung to Nicholas's knee where it rested on the bed below Dave's hip, clung on tight, for he was so breathless he was dizzy with it, or was he simply dizzy with sensation –

He was capable of thought, of small regrets. Wishing he hadn't come already, though he understood why now; he knew Nicholas had been right, it would have been impossible. Wishing he was on his front, on his knees, so that he could feel that delicious arch in his back as he tilted his rear up for Nicholas to plunder –

And this was what it felt like, this plundering, this was what he'd craved, to be part of someone else, for them to be a part of him. "Want more of this –" he said. "I'll want more –"

Nicholas let out a laughing sob, as if happy and relieved and overcome all at once – which Dave supposed he was, really. "Oh my darling man," Nicholas said, reduced to endearments. "My darling David …"

"I want to *know*, I want to learn this."

Nicholas had no words for that, but only gazed down at him, damp–eyed. Meanwhile, his hips maintained a steady rolling rhythm as relentless as the waves on the ocean. Nicholas was almost kneeling upright, one arm tautly stretched before him, the hand clasped around an iron railing of the bed head, his lean bicep a lovely long curve. He was strong, his slim frame and his usual loose clothes were deceptive, though the wide shoulders gave him away. He was strong, and everything a man ought to be. Not who Dave had expected at all. Nicholas's other hand reached down to clasp Dave's hip, keeping them both grounded as he pounded steadily in – careful, but he'd soon realised Dave was coping well enough.

"Next time –" Dave said, each word a pant of precious breath, "wanna be – on hands and knees –"

"Do you … ?" Nicholas seemed to grasp at the conversation now, as if needing distraction. "I'm sorry, I'm selfish, I wanted to be able to see you, to see the gorgeousness."

"You didn't – explain it – that way."

"No," the man admitted with a laugh.

Dave was curled up so far that his shins were against Nicholas's chest, the idea apparently being that he could push Nicholas away if he needed to. His thighs were his strongest muscle group, he knew that, but to be honest he didn't feel strong anywhere right now, he was just heaviness and heat and a whole lot of contradictions such as wanting this to be over and never wanting it to end, or at least not until he had learned it. He was fascinated by the sensations, though he'd hardly call it pleasure, not yet. One day, though, he reckoned. One day he'd grasp it, he'd understand it, and it would make sense, and –

And it would be spectacular.

"I'm sorry," Nicholas was murmuring. Englishmen were always apologising, Dave had found.

"What the fuck for? I was – just thinking – *spectacular*."

Nicholas's colour was already heightened, but he still blushed very prettily about the cheekbones. "I'm sorry you don't have a gorgeous view, as I do."

"You're mad –" Dave told him. "You're beautiful –"

"Oh …" Nicholas groaned raggedly, and sank towards Dave, and struggled a bit, obviously trying to last, but he was overwhelmed. His hand loosened its grip on the railing and dropped to the bed as he leaned in further, and Dave parted his thighs to let him in close, leaned up to meet him as Nicholas drove deeper still with him – and Nicholas came like that, quaking with it, and groaning gutturally as Dave whispered kisses across that beautiful face.

Dave felt that he hardly slept that night. He was happy and delightfully sore, and Nicholas was wrapped close around him, deeply slumbering – and how on earth could Dave sleep? He didn't even need to, he was so happy. The main curtains had been left hanging open, so the first hints of dawn glowing through the net curtains woke Dave from a doze. He lay there contemplating the world and all that was right with it –

And jumped a mile when his mobile went off. Dave reached for it, scrabbled to pick it up from the bedside table, while Nicholas grunted a protest, still mostly asleep. "H'lo?" Dave managed once he'd answered the call. "Denny?"

"Nah, it's Charlie, mate."

"Charlie? God! What is it?" Dave's heart was still thudding in shock, and he had to assume – If anyone was gonna be asked to break bad news to him, it would have to be – *Charlie. What's wrong?*

"Nothing. Nothing's wrong. Just need to talk with you."

Dave let a beat go by, wondering if he was actually dreaming this. None of it was making any sense. "What … ? *Now?*"

"Come on down. I'm outside. Bring your man, if he's awake."

Dave turned to look at Nicholas, but of course he *was* awake by now. His embrace was as encompassing as ever, but he'd lifted his head to listen in. When he caught Dave's eye, he smiled with a soft warmth. Which was very enticing.

"Davey … ?"

Nicholas nodded encouragement, so Dave answered, "All right. Just give us a few minutes."

"You wouldn't make an old man wait while you two got distracted, would you?"

Dave chuckled. "Charlie, we were *asleep*. Give us a few minutes, all right? And I'll try to restrain myself."

"I make no promises," Nicholas added darkly – and Dave ended the call on the sound of Charlie's groan.

But ten minutes later they were walking with Charlie through the cool of early morning towards the Warrego River. After greeting them, Charlie lapsed into silence, so they followed suit. They crossed the river on the Willis Street bridge, walked north–east along the riverbank for a short distance. And then when Charlie indicated, they all settled cross–legged on the ground, underneath a red river gum and beyond that the rich blue sky.

Dave and Nicholas remained quiet, while Charlie thought some more. And then eventually Charlie let his story slowly spill forth.

"That waterhole," said Charlie. "An old friend of mine, he was the last of his tribe to know the songs, to know the story of that place. It has strong magic. Strong."

Well, Dave was on board so far. He exchanged a glance with Nicholas, who obviously agreed.

"He passed those songs on to me, or they would have died with him. So much has been lost already, so many songs forgotten, so many Ancestors go unacknowledged. The power of the land, she's slumbering, but who knows what she will do if the songs aren't ever sung? So it was better that he pass those songs on to someone in the wrong tribe, from the wrong place, than let it all be lost."

They nodded their understanding – though if Charlie was still feeling qualms about it all, then the reassurance of two white guys was hardly going to count for much.

"I went out there," Charlie continued, "I couldn't find it. I walked for days, I couldn't find that place. I was walking round in circles, and old man grunter was having a big laugh."

Into the saddened silence, Dave said, "It's in this wide flat valley. I thought – maybe it's an old crater, you know, formed by a meteorite. But really old, so it's mostly worn down again. Maybe you never saw into the valley, but it's not like it's surrounded by hills or cliffs or anything."

"You found it," Charlie said to Dave.

"Me? Well, both of us."

"Nah, Nicholas found his butterflies. You found the waterhole."

"Well –" But Dave stopped. Nicholas was looking at him intensely, and Charlie was obviously very very serious.

"Long time ago," Charlie mused after a silence had passed, "this was all one land. Gondwanaland. We were all one people. We still are. I'd forgotten that." Another silence, and then Charlie announced, "I'm thinking, I'm still thinking about this, but maybe I need to pass the songs on to you, David Taylor."

He was absolutely astounded. "No … No, that's too much."

"Too much to carry?" Charlie asked, as if testing him.

"Too much honour," Dave protested. "I'm just an ordinary bloke."

"Do you know where you were conceived?"

"Well. Somewhere out here, actually. Mum and Dad had been trying for a while, and she came with him on one of his trips – I guess he was gonna be away for, you know, *those* days. Anyway, he said by the time they got back home they knew already."

Charlie nodded, as if this confirmed it all for him.

"And I was born in Cunnamulla," Dave continued. "Though I wasn't meant to be. Mum didn't come along on many of Dad's trips, but she thought it would be her last chance for a while. And I arrived early."

"Old man grunter chose you," Charlie said, as if there were no point arguing. And maybe there wasn't.

"But, Charlie, it's never done, is it? No one's ever actually passed the really sacred stuff on to a white fella."

"I'm thinking," Charlie said again. "That's all. I haven't even told you the

Ancestor's real name yet. But you should know what I'm thinking."

"Of course," murmured Nicholas. He reached to grasp Dave's hand for a moment, as if to convey his faith.

"I'm gonna talk to the elders about it. They might say no, they might say it's not the Ancestors putting these thoughts in my head. There might be more and more talking, long time arguments. But I won't even start with telling them if you're not willing."

Dave thought about it, but even in the midst of his astonishment he could hardly consider denying Charlie's request. It would mean going back to the waterhole, maybe once a year, maybe more. Learning the songs to sing there, the rituals to perform. He'd make a fool of himself for a while, but there'd be no one to see except Charlie. And in return, there would be a place where he belonged. There would be land that needed him, a song that needed him, no matter how useless he was otherwise.

"If you really think I'm worth it," Dave said.

"The land needs us all," Charlie said in an uncanny echo of Dave's thoughts – and Nicholas took Dave's hand in his again, and this time he didn't let go.

"All right. I mean, of course. Yes," Dave said. "Thank you," he added. Which wasn't anywhere near enough, but was all he had.

He and Nicholas walked back to the hotel together after that, and Dave was so stunned he didn't even realise until they got there that they'd been holding hands the whole way.

twelve

"Can you find your way back there?" Nicholas asked once the satnav flickered and died.

"I'd hope so," said Dave. "I've done this often enough now."

"And it's your land. You have a connection with it."

He quibbled, driving further along the road by instinct. "It's not *my* land. More like, I'm its human. If Charlie's even right."

"I think he's right," Nicholas said. He was obviously still rather awestruck by the whole thing.

So was Dave, come to that, though he retained a scepticism, too. Or a sense of reality, maybe. He suspected the Aboriginal elders Charlie consulted would soon put an end to such notions, and it would all come to very little – well, very little beyond the honour Charlie had done him to even consider such things.

"What do you think?" Nicholas asked, looking around them at the endless scrub. "I feel as if we're close already, but then nothing looks familiar."

"Most people think it all looks the same out here."

"No, there are subtle differences, if you're open to seeing them ..." Nicholas turned to grin at him. "You'd know that better than me."

He returned the grin, but had to shrug. "It's a weird place; it seems to change every time we're here. I have to go on instinct."

"Go on, then."

But actually he had to go against his instincts. It seemed to work if he did the opposite of whatever his sense of direction was telling him. So Dave turned right instead of left off the track, feeling completely mad – and ten minutes later they crested a rise, and drove down into the broader valley.

"You're brilliant," said Nicholas.

At which Dave blushed. He was doing way too much of that lately.

All of Nicholas's clumsiness disappeared when he was having sex, all his uncertainties, and he seemed to completely lack any kind of self–consciousness. The man just took charge and went with it. And Dave found himself more than happy to go along with it, too.

One afternoon Dave found himself on his back on the mattress atop the Cruiser, and his arms were over his head, his hands each wrapped around the roof rack railing. It's just as well he'd chosen the steel, for it was taking all the tension of his flexed arms and stomach as he took most of his own weight. Nicholas was supporting Dave's hips, to an extent, while he knelt there with his thighs wide, powering into Dave as if there were no tomorrow. It was awesome. And the stamina of this guy! This slim Englishman, who had at times seemed so delicate, could come in a moment or last *forever* – and by choice, too.

Afterwards, Dave found that his grip on the railing had kind of locked into place. Nicholas leaned in to help gently prise his fingers back into some semblance of human shape. He pressed a kiss to each one as it was freed.

"Mmm," he murmured as one hand was done and they began work on the other. "Maybe next time I need to tie you down instead."

"Mmm," Dave agreed, finding that he liked the notion – as long as it was understood that Nicholas would then have his thoroughly wicked way with Dave. "Not a chance, though," he had to add.

"Ah, come on," Nicholas chided. "I heard that note of interest in your tone."

"Not while we're out here, mate."

"Why not?"

Dave's hands were both free now. He tentatively stretched them out, and then cradled them on his chest while the blood circulation recovered. "What if something happened to you?"

"I hope something would!" Nicholas retorted.

Dave laughed. "I mean, what if something bad happened to you, and I couldn't free myself? Chances are, you'd fall off the side of the Cruiser, hit your head, and by the time we're found I'd have lost my tackle to sunburn."

Nicholas pondered this disturbing notion. Considered Dave's well–used and well–loved tackle. "Well, we can't have that, can we?"

"No, we can't."

A winsome look turned his way. "So maybe in town … ?"

"Maybe," he agreed. And thought with a rush, *Definitely.*

Even the butterflies seemed to shift to second priority for Nicholas now. The butterflies had laid their eggs – neat rows of little prickly pale green spheres – and Nicholas had taken umpteen dozen photos, but then they just seemed to get on with living. As did Nicholas and Dave.

The two of them spent all their time hanging out together, talking or silent or both of them reading; having ridiculous amounts of sex or lying around idly, randomly touching or sitting quite separately but so very *aware* of each other. They shared the chores around the camp, the cooking and the cleaning and the organising, because no matter how self–indulgent Dave was being otherwise, he wouldn't let such things slip. Nicholas had learned all of Dave's routines by now, and helped without being asked or expecting to be thanked. They worked together well. They did everything together well.

"I know we do," said Nicholas, with the happy kind of smugness that no one could possibly take exception to.

"Oh. Am I thinking out loud again?"

"It's one of your most endearing traits."

"My most idiotic, you mean."

"No, not at all." They were lazing about on the ground near the pool, staying just within the dappled shade provided by the eucalypts. Even so, over time Nicholas's skin had turned a delightfully pale gold colour. All over. Dave dragged his gaze away from the man's narrow rear when Nicholas looked across at him and continued, "I feel that I can always trust you to be yourself. There's never any pretence. None at all."

Dave couldn't help sulking a bit. "Don't wanna be simple …"

"Oh, you're not. You're as complex as anyone. But you're honest, and open. That's marvellous, to me. I think … I suspect it's an Australian thing."

"Dunno." He thought about that for a while. "I guess, maybe. Denise was always – very direct."

"What about your parents? Were they like that?"

"Well, actually my dad was English."

Nicholas sat up with a surprised laugh. "He was?! So you're half English … I didn't know that."

"I've never thought of myself that way. I mean, not that there's anything wrong with that," he added with a grin that Nicholas shared. "But Dad just totally fell in love – with Australia, with my mum, with the Outback. He never went back, not even for a holiday."

"And your mum?"

"Australian. Well, you know. I think the family were originally English and Irish, but they'd come to Brisbane yonks ago. I don't know how many generations, but back into the great–greats, yeah? So what with all of that, I just think of myself as Australian."

Nicholas was nodding emphatically. "And you are, and that's great. But it's cool that we have something in common, isn't it?"

Dave grinned at him, and reached to stroke his fingers across those cheekbones, to push back across his sensitive ears into that thick dark hair. "It's cool that I'm a bit English, too," he agreed. "You're kind of a bit Aussie now."

And they just watched each other for a while, as if they'd never quite get enough.

Eventually, though, Dave cleared his throat. "Um, which town d'you want to go to this time for supplies? I was thinking, maybe we should go back to Woop Woop, so those guys can apologise to you."

Nicholas twisted up his mouth. "Not necessary."

Dave thought some more, but said it anyway: "We can get our own back. We can walk into Drongo Central, holding hands. They won't know *what* to do with themselves."

Nicholas offered him a momentary grin. "Tempting, but no." Then he said, "Why don't we go to Cunnamulla? Your birthplace. You can show me where you were born. Was it at the hospital, or – ?"

"Sentimental idiot," Dave said fondly. At which Nicholas just smiled a bit mysteriously, and winked at him. And Dave found he didn't mind very much at all.

After the Cunnamulla trip worked out, Dave came up with a bolder plan still. "Not the next trip," he suggested while they were still sitting around after dinner one evening, "but maybe the one after? We'll have been out here seven weeks. You'll be just over halfway through your three months. Why don't we do something crazy, like go to Brisbane?"

"Brisbane!" Nicholas repeated, clearly startled.

"It's not so far, if you're up for a day's drive. It's about ten hours from Cunnamulla. We could drive there one day, stay for two nights, then drive back again."

"Oh," the man said. He sat up a bit straighter, and thought about it. "I suppose … I've got used to being out here. It didn't occur to me to go back to the city."

"We could stay at my place," Dave said, suddenly finding that he couldn't quite meet Nicholas's gaze. "I've lived there all my life. My mum and dad bought it when they got married."

"I'd love to see it."

"Won't be anything fancy like you're used to, but I like it. Bit big for one person, mind. It's built in this architectural style – an Australian style called Federation Bungalow. Which isn't as dire as it sounds. It was a bit of a wreck when they bought it – I've got the old photos – but we did it up over the years."

Nicholas was watching him, mouth slightly agape. He stirred himself to say, "I'm sure it's lovely."

"Yeah, well. I belong there, you know?" Dave looked about at their secluded surroundings. "If Charlie's right, and I belong here, then it's as well as there. Cos that's my home."

Nicholas said, with a full heart, "I'd love to stay there with you, even if it is only for two nights."

"*And* … you can meet Denise, maybe."

That earned him a droll look.

"I was an only child, and so was Mum, and so was Dad. So Denise is all the family I have, even if she did drop me."

"I'll be happy to meet her. She sounds – well, like no one I've ever met before."

"Yeah, she is that." Dave laughed. "There. That's what you two have in common. You're like no one I've ever met before, too."

Nicholas sniffed. "I'm sure she'll understand if I think she did an idiotic thing, letting you go."

Dave glared at the man. "Well, that's what you're gonna do, too, isn't it? When you fly back to England?"

Nicholas's head went back, and he turned kind of wild–eyed for a moment. Then: "Yes," he blurted. "I suppose that I will."

Had Nicholas not been thinking that far ahead? Dave sighed. "Well, come on. Might as well make the most of it."

"Carpe diem," said Nicholas after a silent moment. "Seize the day."

"That the Goring family motto, is it?"

"No, actually. Just mine."

Dave knew a joke he could tell, so he played it through once in his head to be sure he had it, then nudged Nicholas's foot with his own to get his attention. "What's the motto of the Fat Poets' Society?"

"What?" Nicholas asked, with a smile dawning.

"Seize the Danish."

"Idiot!" Nicholas said, though he was laughing. He stood, and came over to collect Dave's plate. "Right. Time to do the washing–up."

"Can't it wait this once?" Dave asked, having had other things on his mind.

"Certainly not! David Taylor, I'm shocked at you, letting your standards slide like that."

"All right, all right," he grumbled.

It wasn't long, though, before the chores were done, and they were safely tucked away in their double sleeping bag. Nicholas grabbed at Dave, and dragged him closer. Dave went willingly, letting himself be configured as Nicholas desired.

"Time to make the most of it," Nicholas murmured, and his mouth captured Dave's.

thirteen

Dave didn't think anything of it when he found one of the butterflies lying dead on the ground one afternoon. He supposed that every now and then one would die, just as humans died, naturally or by accident. He felt quite strongly that it should be left to rest in peace at the waterhole, though, and not be added to a collection somewhere, pinned to a board and left in a drawer for months at a time until some stranger came to peer at it. So, feeling a bit guilty and very idiotic, he took it over to the sandier ground by the pool, and quickly scooped out a shallow grave. He laid it quietly within, and pondered for a while the brightness of the blue wings against the reddish soil. But then he heard Nicholas moving about the camp behind him, so Dave quickly covered the butterfly up, and for good measure placed a flat stone over the spot as a mark of respect.

"Sleep well," he whispered. "Go find old man grunter, wherever he's dreaming now …"

"What are you up to?" asked Nicholas in all innocence on Dave's return.

"Just pottering about," said Dave. "Putting things to rights."

And that was so very Dave Taylor that Nicholas didn't question him any further.

Things took a grievous turn a couple of days later. Dave woke rather later than usual, and stretched luxuriously to work the kinks out. He was alone, which was also unusual given that Nicholas tended to just snuggle up even closer if he woke earlier than Dave. He stretched again, senses alert and seeking the scent of tea, the roil of boiling water. Nothing. Nothing, except …

Weeping. Muffled, and resigned rather than distraught, but crying it was. And of course Dave knew who it had to be.

Dave grabbed his shorts and t–shirt, and quickly tugged them on, then swung down the back of the Cruiser, not bothering with the ladder. He'd already spotted Nicholas, on his knees over by the wattle, with his face in his hands. Dave headed over there at a jog.

And he didn't have to ask what the matter was. It was immediately obvious. A drift of dead butterflies, their blue and black wings still deceptively vibrant, trailed across the ground from the wattle back to the edges of the surrounding cliffs. Dave's heart clutched in grief and guilt. "What happened? God, what did we do?" For, despite the fact that he was careful to always wrap up their garbage and take it back to town with him to dispose of, and despite the fact that he always used biodegradable *everything*, Dave assumed that they'd caused this tragedy.

But Nicholas was shaking his head. "Nothing," he managed. "Nothing. This is what happens. Some species barely live even a few days …"

"Ah, mate …" Dave murmured in sorrow and fellow–feeling. He crouched down beside Nicholas, and caught a glimpse of his white tear–sodden face. And Dave forgot about this being a bloke, and thought only of what he'd do when Denise was upset. He shuffled closer, shifting so that Nicholas was bracketed by Dave's legs, and then Dave tugged him close so he could hold him.

Nicholas, unsurprisingly, collapsed against him, and Dave sat there cradling him for a while, stroking gently at his back and shoulders and hair. Dave had time to remember how cold–blooded Nicholas had seemed when taking specimens of his beautiful butterflies; so different to how he was now, confronted by natural mortality. Perhaps Nicholas could explain that, or perhaps not. Dave knew all too well that death and grieving could affect people in such different ways.

Eventually Nicholas quietened, but he didn't seem to want to move, and Dave was hardly going to make him. So Dave had time to remember the lone dead butterfly he'd found, and he wondered if that had been *their* butterfly, the first to emerge, the one that welcomed them to the waterhole and had seemed so keen to drink from Dave's skin. Of course it would have reached the end of its natural lifespan sooner than the rest.

When Nicholas finally stirred and sat up, Dave offered him a gentle smile, and received a wobbly one in return. "Shall I make some tea?" Dave asked. "Or … anything. What would you like to do?"

"Tea." Nicholas nodded. He glanced away for a moment, chewing on his lower lip in thought. Then he looked back at Dave. "I'd like to tell you something. If you don't mind."

"Of course. You can tell me anything." Dave shifted, and stretched out his left leg which had gone to sleep. "All right for now, mate?"

"Yes. Thank you." Another watery smile. "I'll be along in a minute. I'll wash my face. I must look a sight."

"Beautiful as ever, I'm afraid," Dave said stoutly. "You are *so* bad for my peace of mind." And Nicholas even laughed a little under his breath at such a ridiculous notion.

"I have – I have a brain aneurysm." Nicholas's face was long and chalk–white. "I'll save you from all the details of what's happened, and how they found it, but –"

"Oh Nicholas!" Dave quietly burst out once he'd regained his voice.

Nicholas blinked, and carried on. "– but I could drop dead at any time, or have a stroke, or what have you. There's no predicting it, and very little preventative treatment available. The risks of surgery are about the same as the risks of not doing anything, so I decided not to. Do anything."

A stunned silence grew.

Dave struggled for something to say. Eventually he came up with: "Is that what the medication's for?"

"Yes. It's nothing exotic. It controls my blood pressure. Which should reduce the risk of –" But apparently he couldn't bring himself to say it twice.

"This is awful," Dave managed, which was horribly inadequate, but what else was there to say? Nicholas was only two or three years older than Dave himself. Otherwise healthy men in their twenties shouldn't have to face this kind of thing. Dave tried to think it through. "Is that why –"

"Yes," Nicholas said, cutting him off. "I expect it's the explanation for a lot of things."

Dave felt at a complete loss.

Then suddenly it was far far easier to feel angry. It helped him ignore the great gaping chasm that had opened up right under his feet. "Why the hell didn't you tell me?" he asked – not loud, but furious. "You might have died out here, and I wouldn't know why, or what to do –"

"There's nothing you could do," Nicholas crisply replied. "Or not that you wouldn't have done anyway. Simon made sure that you're qualified to apply first aid. You would have called for an air ambulance, and tried to resuscitate me."

"Yeah, thanks," said Dave, laying on the irony.

"I left a letter – with the medication. You or the medical personnel would have looked for the medication, and found the letter. There's nothing more you could have done."

"I don't believe you. Telling me might have made the difference between you dying and … and you *not* dying."

"Well," came the tart response. "Under some circumstances, I think I would actually rather die."

Dave just stared at the man, infuriated by the situation he could have – he could *still* find himself in. But he understood, too. Reluctantly, he had to admit that a part of him did understand. Nicholas didn't want this condition to define his life.

"Exactly. I was tired of – of being taken care of. In relation to my health, anyway. And – well. I might live until something else gets me, or I might not have much time. I don't know. But I wanted to do this, to find the butterflies. I didn't want to risk you deciding that you couldn't bring me out here."

And he really did understand. Dave hated that. It went against all his rules, but he couldn't help thinking he'd have probably done the same.

"Thank you," Nicholas said stiffly. "I do appreciate the position I might have put you in."

"Thanks," said Dave, very quietly, but he meant it this time.

"And once you've forgiven me, I can assure you …" Nicholas caught Dave's eye, and glanced towards their bed on top of the Cruiser. "Regular exercise is to be encouraged."

"Oh, *Nicholas*," Dave said brokenly. He was breaking apart inside from anticipated grief.

And as with their first real kiss, Dave couldn't say now who initiated it – but what did that matter? A moment later they were sitting on the ground between the two chairs, and Dave was cradling Nicholas again, who curled up within his arms and clung on. It seemed that Nicholas was done crying for now, but of course he still needed the comfort.

All Dave could think was that, no matter what Nicholas was to Dave, whether he was a client or a friend – and no matter if they never saw each other again after this trip – Dave liked the world a whole lot better for knowing that Nicholas was in it.

"Thank you," Nicholas said again, almost gasping.

"Is this why –" Dave dared to ask. "Is this why the butterflies?"

"Tell me."

"They make you feel long–lived."

"Positively ancient," Nicholas agreed. "And … ?"

But he was all out of wisdom. "Tell me," said Dave.

Nicholas sighed. He was almost calm again now. "Because … you can hibernate a very long time in that chrysalis. But once you emerge –"

"You become fabulous," Dave supplied.

Nicholas shifted around so that he could see Dave properly. "But then the clock starts ticking."

They took it slow. They drank the tea, which had remained warm in its pot. And then Dave took Nicholas back to their bed. This time, Dave made love to the man. And he treated him as gently as he knew how.

"There," said Nicholas afterwards, sounding philosophical. "We hit the high point."

Don't, Dave wanted to say. But who was he to deny Nicholas anything?

"It was one of those dangerous moments," Nicholas said, obviously quoting something, *"when feeling, running high above its average depth, leaves flood–marks which are never reached again."* He sighed again. "Denise would recognise that."

Don't. Dave hid his face against Nicholas's throat, cheek against the steady thrum of his heartbeat, and he held on to the man with tender strength.

"Do you know what the name David means?" Nicholas asked a long while later. When Dave shook his head, Nicholas answered, "Beloved."

"What does Nicholas mean?"

"Virile," the man claimed.

Dave stared at him for a long moment, before bursting into laughter. "It does not!"

"It does, actually."

"Prove it!"

"I'd love to." And Nicholas rose up from the mattress like a whale breaching the surface of the ocean, and then he turned, and took Dave under.

fourteen

They reached Dave's house around seven–thirty one evening. Dave smiled as he walked in the front door: he liked being home. And his smile broadened as he welcomed Nicholas in.

"There's a side door off the garage," he explained inconsequentially, "but I thought you'd better see it properly. At least the first time."

"It's lovely," Nicholas said as he trailed along behind Dave, gazing about him as Dave turned on the lights in the hallway, then the living room. Dave himself looked about at the colours with fresh eyes – the dark green, and rich cream, and occasional scraps of rusty red – before leading Nicholas through into the family room and kitchen. "Now, *this* is nice," Nicholas added appreciatively, as he took in the room that ran along two–thirds of the width of the house.

"Wait until you see it in the morning," Dave said. "There's a veranda out the back there, and then the yard. This is the best room …" He grinned, and then pointed in the direction of the other third of the back of the house. "Well, this and the master bedroom, anyway."

Nicholas's smile curled wickedly. "I trust you'll give me the full tour later." And he didn't mean the house.

"I'll just check the fridge –" Though why he even said that, Dave had no idea. He knew he could rely on Denise, and there was no point in pretending to Nicholas that she wasn't an intrinsic part of his life. "We've got the essentials here, Denise said she'd make sure of that. Thought I'd make an omelette for dinner, if that's all right."

"That's great."

Dave started fetching out the eggs and butter, mushrooms and capsicum, bacon and cheese. "D'you wanna get cleaned up, or anything?"

"Later," Nicholas said. "Is the shower big enough for both of us?"

Dave went pink. "Maybe …"

"Then the shower can wait for afterwards. I'll make a pot of tea, if I may. You do the sustenance, I'll do the antioxidants."

"Going to need them, are we?"

"Oh yes," said Nicholas. And once the tea was stewing, he sat there at the breakfast bar, watching Dave with a wickedly content smile.

They weren't expected at Denise's until twelve–thirty, so after coffee and muesli, and a wander around the lushly planted backyard, the two of them seemed to gravitate quite naturally again to bed.

"Making the most of it?" Dave asked as he backed towards the bed, with Nicholas's hands sliding up under his t–shirt.

"Seize the Dave," Nicholas whimsically agreed.

Dave laughed – but then Nicholas turned serious, reaching around Dave to tug at the doona and then fling it off the bed and onto the floor with a strong twist of his wrist. Dave was pushed back to fall against the mattress, the cotton sheet cool against his skin. Nicholas eyed the wooden slats of the bed for a moment, before turning back to Dave. "What can I tie you down with?"

Dave let out a gasp, and he instinctively wriggled away on his elbows and rear – until Nicholas caught him again with one long pale hand wrapped around Dave's ankle.

"What can I use?" Nicholas demanded.

"Dad's dressing gown belt," Dave blurted.

"Good," said Nicholas. And he headed for the wardrobe that Dave indicated with a nod. "Good," he said again, once he'd found it.

Nicholas walked back towards the bed, his gaze pinning Dave down. And Dave's cock kicked into full–blooded life.

It was nothing like he'd expected.

Dave found himself naked and face down on the bed, the wrong way round with his head towards the foot, and his arms free. His ankles, however, were bound together and then the tie was secured to the bed head. Nicholas was sitting there against the pillows, just looking at him lying there. Nothing else seemed to be happening at all.

"Uh …" Dave started uncertainly.

"Hush," said Nicholas. One of his cool hands wrapped again around Dave's ankle, and caressed him through the binding. "Let me see you," he continued.

Dave shifted to look at him over his shoulder. "What?"

"Shush … Put your head back down. Then arch the small of your back the way you like to. Show me that *delicious* arch in your back."

"Oh …" he groaned. He was sure he'd never talked about that. Nicholas must have really been paying attention. After a moment Dave shifted back a little so he could do as Nicholas requested – which of course meant that his rear was poking up in the air. He assumed that was the intention.

"Further," said Nicholas. "I want you to really feel it."

He did so, forcing the curve until it was just the right side of painful.

"Good." That hand patted at his calf in reward. "Now show yourself to me. No, keep your knees together, but turn your thighs and your rear out. I want to see everything you've got."

Dave mumbled something that was half a protest, but he did his best to obey, though it felt to be an infinitesimal move. Nicholas, however, again expressed his appreciation.

"Now," said Nicholas. "Don't move. Not even a twitch."

"But –"

"What did I tell you?"

"Don't move," he said with a sigh. He didn't know how he'd go with that, though. Even when he let Nicholas do all the driving, Dave still liked to participate, and he still liked to be working his hips when he came.

"Good."

"I'll try –"

"You won't move. You will, however, give thought to coming like this. Without me touching your cock." Nicholas continued on, overriding anything Dave was about to say: "I'm going to be rimming you and fingering you, and sucking on your balls, and fucking you – and you're going to come."

"But –"

"Hush …" Nicholas was shifting, and apparently stalking down the bed until he could straddle Dave's legs on all fours without touching him – until he bit gently at the curve of Dave's butt.

Dave's breath hitched. And thus began an endless time of torment.

At the last, Nicholas took mercy on him, and reached below to take him in hand, to end it with three masterful strokes. Which triggered an orgasm almost too intense to be pleasurable.

"I'm sorry," Dave was mumbling afterwards, as Nicholas unfastened him. The man didn't make Dave move, but brought a pillow down with him and tucked it under Dave's head, tugged the doona up over them both, and then wrapped himself around Dave as if he'd never ever be pried off. "I'm sorry."

"What for?" Nicholas asked, sounding immensely satisfied. "*God*, that was good."

"I'm sorry I couldn't come like you wanted."

"Oh, my darling man! You didn't have to. It was just an idea. I'm sorry you felt you had to."

"I wanted to. I wanted to cos you wanted it."

"I know, you gorgeous thing. Hush now. Let's have a nap, and then we'll get cleaned up again. All right?"

"All right," said Dave. And he sank away into warm velvety darkness.

Of course they were late for lunch, and of course Denise knew exactly why. She greeted Dave with a smirk and an unexpected kiss on the cheek. "Hello, Davey." She took a moment to look him over, before handing him Zoe. "You're looking well. Not to mention well–shagged."

"Jeez, Denise!" he grumbled, feeling his face flame up again. He sought refuge in a much safer topic. "How's little Zo?" he asked, cradling the sleepy warm figure in both arms. "She's, like, twice as big as when I last saw her."

"Yeah, she's doin' great. You must be Nicholas," Denise added, reaching past Dave to shake Nicholas's hand.

"I'm pleased to meet you, Denise."

"Oh yeah, sorry," Dave said. But they were taking care of the introductions without him, which was just as well.

But then when Dave started drifting towards the family room, he found that the others weren't quite done yet. Denise and Nicholas were actually standing there in the hallway, sizing each other up.

"You know," said Denise, "I don't want to make you feel uncomfortable or anything, but I only invited you around to make sure you're good enough for him."

Nicholas scoffed a laugh in a manner befitting an honorary Australian. "That's all right. I only accepted to make sure you know he's not yours anymore."

"Guys –" Dave said, heading back there. Zoe was stirring in his arms, as if picking up on the tensions.

But eventually Denise simply said, "I know that."

"Do you?"

"Well, I do now," Denise replied with a laugh. She offered to shake hands again. "You'll do, Nicholas."

"Thank you, Denise."

Dave sighed. "Right. Thank God that's over."

Luckily Vittorio seemed nothing more than amused by these two squaring off over Dave – and Dave had long ago realised that Vittorio wasn't the jealous type. As Denise and Vittorio headed for the kitchen, Dave and Nicholas followed after to settle at the table in the family room. Vittorio brought them a bottle of Cascade each. And Dave had time to belatedly feel flattered. No one else in all these years had ever thought Dave worth challenging Denise for. But still. They weren't in high school anymore. Dave hoped that was that.

Denise brought a warmed–up bottle of milk over for him to feed Zoe with, and got him properly started. The baby gazed up at him solemnly as she settled into it. Meanwhile, Denise and Vittorio were finishing off their preparations for lunch, and asking Nicholas about his trip; Nicholas was telling them about the butterflies as if he were a relatively sane person. Everything was going suspiciously well.

When Zoe got to the end of the bottle, Dave put it down, and then considered her for a long moment. She wriggled a bit uncomfortably, and he knew he was meant to do something else with her at this point, not have her lying back in his arms. "Is this the bit when I chuck her over my shoulder, or something?"

Denise had her hands full of crockery, and quickly spun about to put it back down – though Vittorio was inadvertently in the way. "Hang on," she said. Zoe scowled forebodingly.

"Not *over* your shoulder," Nicholas was advising. "A bit more civilised than that." He was standing by Dave now, laying a hand towel over Dave's shoulder – and then, with his hands cradling Dave's, showing him exactly how to hold Zoe upright against his chest, with her head lightly supported. "There you go. Now pat her back gently."

Denise was just watching them, obviously approving. "Kids of your own?"

she asked Nicholas.

"Oh no," he answered with a smile. "More nieces and nephews than I can count. It's only my eldest brother living at home now, with his wife and children, but we see a great deal of the others." He sat down again as he rambled on. "If there's a good kids' movie on, I get to borrow whoever will come with me to see it at the cinema. Or they'll stay over on a Saturday night, and I get to babysit while their parents go out – which really means I just get to hang out with them. That sort of thing."

Denise smiled. "You'll do very nicely indeed, Nicholas Goring."

A remark seconded by a resounding burp from Zoe, and backed up with a great deal of laughter.

The two of them walked slowly back to Dave's place, Nicholas looking as adorable as ever in his Akubra.

"I'm glad I got you that hat," said Dave.

"I am, too," Nicholas answered with simple sincerity.

They wandered on, watching each other a bit skittishly. Dave began to fear another hand–holding incident was imminent – and was relieved when his phone chimed to announce the distraction of a text message. Though he groaned when he read it. *You're in love with your earling.* Denise, of course.

Dave made sure the display was hidden from Nicholas. *I am not. Go away! Are too. Can't fool me, Davey.*

He turned the thing to silent, and shoved it back in his pocket. Cleared his throat and said to Nicholas, "Shall we go do the grocery shopping for next week? Get that done?"

"It can wait for tomorrow, can't it?"

"Guess so. If you don't mind it being a long day, with the drive as well."

"Don't worry about that. I'm feeling rather like seizing the Dave again."

"Oh," he said, unable to prevent a pleased smile giving everything away. It was just as well no one was about on this warm afternoon, for surely this was worse than holding hands.

As it turned out, Nicholas didn't seize him at all, but instead treated him sweetly and gently, as if Dave needed seducing. It was lovely.

Later that evening, after they'd eaten dinner and were sprawled on the lounge watching TV, Nicholas said, "Don't worry about tomorrow. We're not going back."

Dave was so startled, that all he could do was repeat, "We're not –"

"No," said Nicholas very evenly. "I've changed my ticket. I'm flying back to England tomorrow."

Dave's hand was clutching painfully at Nicholas's, but the man didn't flinch or indeed show anything much. "What?" Dave managed. "No …"

"I'm no good at farewells. At this point, I'd rather take the coward's way out and go home."

"No. No, you *can't.*"

"I am, though. At least I'm telling you today. It's hard enough living with the goodbye for a few hours. I can't do it for a few weeks."

"But –" It wasn't just about Dave. It was about the whole trip. "You haven't finished with the butterflies yet! The trip's barely half over!"

Nicholas cleared his throat. "The balance of your fee will be in your account by now. Simon's taking care of it."

"God, d'you really think I care about the money?"

"No, I don't suppose that you do. But I care about upholding my end of a deal."

"Is *that* what you think you're doing?" Dave demanded – immediately continuing, "You haven't finished with the butterflies. You haven't seen the caterpillars yet."

"But we don't know when that will be. They might only go through one life cycle each year. Even if the eggs don't have a dormant phase, they might take weeks to hatch. We could go back and spend over a month doing nothing but watching the eggs."

"Doing nothing … ?" he protested.

"David, it's done. My flight leaves around one in the afternoon. I'll take a taxi to the airport, if you'd prefer. In fact, I'll take a taxi now, if you like, and stay at a hotel for the night."

"Don't be ridiculous!" Dave burst out.

"Well, don't make this any harder than it needs to be."

Dave fell silent, and let the man's hand go. This was horrible. Dave felt as if he'd ruined everything. But he also felt that Nicholas had wilfully let it be ruined. Though the man had enough to be dealing with already, and no doubt he was doing the best he could. They were both just doing the best they could, weren't they? Dave sighed.

"I don't understand," he said. "What do you mean about not being good at farewells?"

"Just exactly that. I don't have the art of saying goodbye. Not gracefully. Normally, I don't let things start – not really – so that I don't have to say goodbye at the end." Nicholas reached to take Dave's hand in his again. "I broke all my rules for you."

"Then we're even, aren't we," said Dave. "Just … talk to me. I want to understand. And give it to me straight. I reckon I already have abandonment issues, so don't worry about that."

"Oh, *David,*" Nicholas said with a wry fondness.

"Is this about … the last goodbye? The final one?"

"Well. Yes. I almost – don't want to start living, because I can't face it ending. Being alone – other than my family – It makes the prospect of letting go – easier."

"Ah, no … No, mate."

"Tell me another way. There is no other way. It can't be another way."

"I get it," said Dave. "I do. But it's too late. You *are* living. You've transformed. You're the fabulous butterfly now."

"Because of you," Nicholas suggested with a half–sceptical half–pleased little smile.

"No, you already were when you met me. You just didn't know it yet."

"Oh God," Nicholas said, with his breath shuddering for a moment. "David. This has been –"

"I know," said Dave, cutting him off, terrified that they'd both end up bawling like babies. "I know."

And Nicholas pushed over to kiss him, and then he really did seize Dave, and they fucked, right there on the lounge. Frantically.

They eventually made it to Dave's bed, and Nicholas abruptly fell deeply asleep. He was exhausted, and perhaps taking the coward's way out in this as well. David didn't blame him at all, even while he lay awake, already feeling lonely.

The following morning, they were polite to each other, in a friendly enough way. They didn't fuck again. Nicholas took his time repacking his gear, which didn't really need it. He'd obviously been at least half intending to do this all along. Dave helped him, and fed him, made him coffee, and watched him, keeping his distance, as required.

He found himself wishing that Nicholas would say something – any little thing – to indicate that they might meet again. A hint of plans for another trip next year to see the butterflies. An invitation to drop by if Dave should ever find himself in England. Anything like that. But no. Nicholas talked about practicalities, but was otherwise quiet – not reminiscing about the trip, and not looking ahead to anything beyond his flight.

Soon enough, they had to leave so that Nicholas had time for all the international check–in procedures.

Soon enough – too soon – it was time to part. Once Nicholas was beyond the security barriers, then he was as good as out of the country.

"Just tell me you don't hate me," Nicholas said as they stood there together.

"For what?"

Nicholas shrugged. "Just tell me. Lie if you have to."

Dave looked at him, steady and true. "I don't hate you."

"Thank you," Nicholas said. And there in Departures, with everyone milling around them, Nicholas pressed one last kiss to Dave's mouth. And Dave didn't hate him for that, either. "Goodbye, David."

"Goodbye," he whispered.

Nicholas turned, and resolutely headed for the security entrance. He turned left into the corridor with his head high and one last glance that barely even made it halfway towards Dave. A moment later the man was gone.

fifteen

Dave felt at a total loss. He took care of the Cruiser and its contents that afternoon – clearing everything out, cleaning it, reorganising, noting what needed restocking, and all the rest of it. He bought himself some groceries, and caught up with his laundry.

He gave hours of serious thought to going back out to the waterhole by himself. Surely he owed it to Nicholas to go and record the hatching of the eggs, and the … the crawling of the caterpillars. Even if it was taking a while, he could probably go back every couple of weeks or so, just to keep an eye on developments. After all, if Dave hadn't broken his own rules, then Nicholas would still be here, they'd be client and tour guide – with some tensions, perhaps, and probably not friends as they'd become – and his client wouldn't have felt the need to cut his trip short, and maybe could even have extended it if he'd needed to. If the butterflies really weren't cooperating.

But the thought of going back there right away on his own just filled him with reluctance. He felt an almost physical resistance to the idea. Dave had been alone for so long that he'd gotten used to it. Before his unexpected English earling had turned up, anyway. Now he thought that hanging around that waterhole without Nicholas to share it with would crush him with loneliness.

Not that hanging around home was going to be much better, he supposed. He'd have to start calling around the travel agents and tourist centres, and let them know that he was available again for short or long trips. He'd have to get used to the notion of having other people to take care of. He'd have to relearn how to keep a professional distance.

Dave sighed, and headed back inside. The scent of Nicholas and sex still lingered in his bed, so Dave grabbed a pillow and took it through to the lounge with him. Wore away the night hours with television. Which wasn't an answer, but it got him through the first day.

Or maybe, he found himself reflecting on the second day, he could have broken his fraternisation rules but handled it all better so that Nicholas hadn't panicked and felt the need to leave. There must have been some way to reassure the man that they could part with a laconic Aussie 'see ya' rather than a solemn English 'goodbye'. That way, they could have had five more weeks of sex and friendship and – well, Dave had to acknowledge the truth – affection. Surely he could have managed that.

He was obviously totally useless at relationships, whether short or long.

He lay low for most of that first week, pottering about the house and working on the garden. Reading *The Reverse of the Medal* and *The Letter of Marque.*

And then he finally went around to see Denise.

She was astonished, to say the least, to find him on her doorstep. And all the more so to find him alone. "Davey! Why aren't you out at your waterhole? And what have you done with Nicholas?"

He explained, as best he could, at the dining table over a mug of coffee. He kept his voice low, and avoided both dire curses and airy denials, because Zoe was asleep in a bassinet just around the corner in the living room. Not that he needed to curse or deny. It had ended badly, which was probably to be expected given that he'd made so many mistakes. But that was that, and Dave just had to get used to being alone again.

"Oh, *Davey* …" Denise said in sorrowful tones, reaching to wrap his hand in hers.

He didn't need sympathy. He took his hand away and drank his coffee.

"Nicholas was trying to do the right thing by you," she said rather more coolly.

"Yeah, absolutely …" he said, voice heavy with sarcasm.

"You probably made it clear to him that it was only a holiday fling."

"It *was* only a holiday fling."

"Oh, for God's sake!" she said, sitting back and rolling her eyes. "So what's with all the moping now?"

Dave glared at her. "Cos he just left! Five weeks early! And I stuffed everything up, I ruined his trip for him, I should have known better than to break my rules, and he was bloody–minded enough to pay the fee for the whole three months as well!"

Denise sighed. "From what I saw of Nicholas, I'd say he had the time of his life out there with you. Perhaps he wanted to end it on a high note."

"I don't see how that's doing the right thing by me."

"Oh you idiot, do you really not get it? You're such a loveable sort, Davey. We all want to take care of you. Your dad, me. Nicholas. We try to do what's right for you."

"Leaving wasn't right for me." He frowned, and amended that: "Not yet, anyway. Obviously he was going to leave later."

"If you were really so determined that it was only for the three months and no longer, then you can hardly blame him for ending it on his own terms. Poor sod."

That earned her another glare. "I should have known you'd take his side in this."

"Davey, don't be any more idiotic than you have to be."

"Look," he said stiffly. "I have found that … nothing lasts forever."

"If that's the only thing I taught you, Davey, then I'm more sorry than I can say. But it's not, is it?"

He set his face against her at the time, and in a thoroughly disgruntled mood Dave left and walked home again. Wondering what the hell to do next.

But it didn't take him long to back down a bit. Fair's fair, he thought. So he texted her: *Not the only thing.*

Charlie called the next day, and was almost totally convincing in claiming that Denise hadn't put him up to it. "Nah, mate, I'm coming up to Brisbane for a few days. Thought we should have a beer."

"Come and stay," Dave offered. "The house is too big since Dad died."

"So … what have you done with your man, Davey?"

"He's gone back to England. As I'm sure you know already."

"Then you're going, too?"

"No." Dave frowned over that. Of course he'd thought about it. He just figured there wasn't any point. If this was the way that Nicholas wanted it, then who was Dave to argue?

"Davey … ?" Charlie prompted after what must have been a lengthy silence.

"Look," said Dave. "I reckon you know he thinks he doesn't have long, right? Well, I think he just wants to live his life his way, the best he can."

"His way would be with you, mate."

"No, I think he wants to keep it easy. I think he wants to spare himself, and whoever else … the grief." God, even saying it brought an intimation of the weight of it down upon him.

"We're all going to die, Dave my man. No reason not to live while we can. There'll be time enough in the Dreaming for the rest."

"Well, then," Dave argued, "it can wait. Can't it?"

"No, what you have with Nicholas is a part of life. The kind of thing you *do* get to take with you when you go, if you live it right. Next thing I want to hear about you, my man, is that you're in England."

"But I don't think he really wants –"

"I never knew you for a fool, David Taylor."

"Oh." After a moment he rallied again. "Well, I can't, can I? What about the waterhole? And the songs?"

"You'll come back," Charlie said, in his confident way. The man had such faith! "I'm thinking both of you will be back, and you'll be looking after that place for us, Nicholas will be looking after those butterflies. And the grunter and his love will be together again."

Dave sank a bit, overwhelmed. Minutes went by, but "Oh" was all he managed to say. And then, weakly, "I can't."

"All right," Charlie said easily. "Well, I'll see you in a week or so. If you come to your senses, though, just call me. I can find somewhere else to stay."

"You won't have to."

"We'll see."

Right. He really hated it when people said that.

And of course, Denise wouldn't leave the subject alone. "You're not *that* embarrassed about being with a guy, are you? Life's too short, Davey."

He almost laughed at that. "His motto was Seize the Day."

"Well … ?"

"It's not that I minded being with a bloke as such …"

"You minded being his bitch."

Dave went bright red, and thanked God or the Ancestors that Vittorio wasn't around. "Denise!"

"If that's how things are between you –"

She meant the sex, he assumed. "It's not *that* I mind so much as –"

"People knowing."

"Yes."

"Everyone knew you were my bitch, Davey, and you lived with it."

All right, that gave him pause. "Yeah, I did, didn't I?" The endless jokes about who wore the trousers in their relationship had been so much a part of his life that they'd never bothered him. As a child he'd always wondered what on earth could have been so wrong with enjoying Denise taking care of him. As a man, he'd understood better, but still he felt that most people who'd teased him about it had just been jealous.

"So what's different?" she asked.

He thought about it some more, and couldn't come up with an answer.

Denise realised, of course, that she was finally making some headway. She came to sit next to him, and just spoke very gently now. Not pushing at all. "I almost bought what you said at first, about it being a short–term thing. But I don't anymore."

He looked at her doubtfully. But underneath, his whole world was shifting.

"Maybe he was wrong, but he was trying to look after you, Davey. Now it's your turn to look after him – and yourself, too. *You* have to seize the day this time. He can't do it all on his own."

"Denny –"

"You've got to go find him again. You've got to go get your man!"

"That sort of thing," he said a bit shakily, "it only happens in books. Movies."

She emphatically disagreed. "No. You go make it happen in real life, too."

And in that moment, he knew he would. He wasn't quite ready yet. But he knew.

"And send me an invite, won't you?" Denise added.

"For what?"

"Your wedding."

"What?"

"You can get married over there, you know. I want to be – I *demand* to be your best man."

"Denny –"

"You were mine."

"Oh God …"

And so once he'd escorted the Americans around in their quest to wrestle crocodiles, the next trip that Dave prepared for was to Buckinghamshire in England. He decided it had better be a surprise. If he was going to be dropped all over again, it had better be made clear and done in person. He wouldn't know what to do if he contacted Nicholas and then received an ambivalent email in response that could be interpreted a hundred different ways. Dave didn't want to lose what little certainty he had.

He knew for sure he was doing the right thing before he flew out, though. Because he was browsing the internet on his mobile while hanging around the departure lounge at the Brisbane airport. And he happened to Google 'Nicholas Goring'. And the first entry in the search results was from the website of *The Australian Journal of Entomology*, announcing an article that would appear in the following month's issue. It was about an Englishman, and the new butterfly he'd discovered in the Outback.

And he'd called the butterfly *Ogyris davidi*: David's Azure.

sixteen

Dave was standing at the massive doorway to a manor house, feeling somewhat overwhelmed. Definitely about to change his mind and take the coward's way out. It was a gentle English summer afternoon. Somewhere there were children laughing in irrepressible delight – perhaps in the gardens. Which was lovely, and brought this imposing old house alive. They were some of Nicholas's nieces and nephews, Dave assumed. The sound was magical, but it also underlined the fact that Dave didn't really belong there.

His hand, which had been about to ring the bell again, fell loosely to his side.

Dave had just turned away when the door finally opened – and the very proper butler, after a long moment, softened into a happy smile. "Mr Taylor … ? Yes, it is, isn't it? I recognise you from your photo. I'm sorry to have kept you waiting."

"Hello, Simon," Dave replied.

"Please, do come in. You'll be very welcome, sir."

"David."

"Thank you, David. I'll take you through to the conservatory. You'll be able to surprise him there."

A blur of rooms, and then they were there already, before Dave had even had time to catch his breath.

"Nicholas? You have a visitor."

Dave just stood there, still within the darkness of the house proper, a little way behind Simon, unable to really take much in. Nicholas was there in the gentle plant–filtered sunlight, sitting cross–legged on a tarpaulin on the tiled floor, potting orchids. With someone beside him. A child. That was all right. Dave's heart was pounding.

Nicholas stared for a moment, and then unfolded to stand with his usual inelegant grace. "David?" he said, in a hushed tone – not confirming who he was, of course, but really asking The Question. *Will you … ?*

"Yes," Dave answered huskily. *For better or worse, as long as we both shall live.* "Will you … ?" he asked. *Come live with me and be my love – in Australia.*

"Yes." Then Nicholas closed the remaining distance between them with two shaky strides, and Dave was deep in his arms, and holding on with all his might, and they were kissing kissing *kissing*, and it was just the most *awesome* thing …

Until they were recalled to their surroundings by the giggle of a child and the clearing of a butler's throat.

"Oh," said Nicholas, stepping back a little. "Well. How are you?" he asked, running a caressing hand back over Dave's hair. "Did you come straight here? What a long journey you must have had, that flight is hellish, isn't it – I'm sure you're parched. Simon, please would you bring us some tea?"

"Yes, sir, of course."

"Here, come and meet my nephew Robin," Nicholas continued, taking Dave by the hand and leading him out into the conservatory. "We're just re-potting these orchids, but we'll be done soon. You can help us, if you like."

"Sure," Dave said, starting to let go and relax into the flow of it. Nicholas would take care of him, he knew that now. He could trust this man with *everything*.

"Robin, this is my friend David, from Australia."

"Pleased to meet you, sir."

"You, too, Robin."

"I should warn you that *everyone's* here," Nicholas said as he sank back down to the tarpaulin. Dave sat down beside him, infinitely comfortable despite everything. "A gathering of Gorings. It's the summer holidays, you see. But you don't have to meet them all yet. We'll have tea first, and get you unpacked …" Nicholas's gaze caressed him, top to toe, adding the promise of *undressed … debauched …* "Not that you should worry. Everyone's going to be so glad you came."

At last Nicholas was quiet again, and after a while Dave felt he should offer something more. "I'm glad, too," he said, his voice still rusty as if he hadn't used it, not properly, for so very long.

"How brave you've been. How incredible!" And Nicholas took one of Dave's hands in his, and lifted it to caress Dave's palm with his cheek. "Thank you, David. Thank you so much."

"Nnn," he replied, quite coherently.

What with one thing and the other, it was a couple of hours before they headed back down to meet everyone. As they reached the top of the stairs,

Dave asked, "Are you sure I'm dressed well enough?" He was in a new pair of washed–out blue jeans, and a white button–down shirt in a textured cotton which he wore loose, and brown leather sandals. The outfit had cost him so much that he winced to remember, but now all he could think was that he must appear too casual.

"How someone as gorgeous as you can fret about what he's wearing, I have no idea," Nicholas grumbled. "As if anyone is even going to notice! And anyway, it's not like we do the whole white–tie–and–tails thing for dinner."

"Oh God. You know, I've never even *worn* a suit in my whole life … ?"

"All right, now *that's* a deal–breaker, if ever I heard one." They'd reached the landing, from which the staircase swept down into the main hall. Nicholas stopped, and tugged gently at Dave's hand to bring him round to face him. "Let me have another look at you, then …" His gaze caressed Dave once more from top to toe, making Dave blush yet again. "You look *perfect:* you look exquisitely yourself."

He mumbled something grateful, and then they continued on down the stairs …

Only to find that they must have been overheard, for two men were sitting on the pair of sofas either side of the fireplace down there, apparently talking quietly between themselves. They stood as Nicholas changed tack and approached the men.

"My father and brother," Nicholas had a moment in which to murmur to Dave – and then they were there, and Dave was being formally presented. "Father, may I introduce my friend David Taylor, from Australia. David, this is my father, Lord Goring."

"It is a great pleasure to meet you, David, and to welcome you to our home."

"Thank you, my lord," he managed smoothly enough as they shook hands. "It's a real honour to be here."

"Please call me Richard; we don't stand on ceremony with friends." And he certainly seemed to be a delightfully avuncular figure.

"Thank you," said Dave, half of his fears melting away already.

"Robert," Nicholas continued to the other man, who looked like a rather less beautiful, rugby–playing version of Nicholas himself, "this is my friend David. David, this is my eldest brother, Robert."

Again they shook hands, and did the "Very happy to meet you, David" – "Thank you, my lord" – "Thanks, but please call me Robert" exchange.

As the three Gorings chatted briefly about some household business or other, and as the happy sounds of a large family gathering floated faintly through from elsewhere in the house, it occurred to Dave that the earl and his heir had deliberately positioned themselves here in order to greet Dave, and ease him into this whole meet–the–family thing. Which was beyond considerate. Dave relaxed a little more, beginning to anticipate that he faced nothing worse now than confusion about which names belonged to which newly met faces. But he had Simon and Robin, Richard and Robert sorted out already, and Nicholas of course. Always and forever Nicholas.

"Shall we go in?" Richard asked. "If I introduce David as your friend, Nicholas, is that acceptable to you both?"

"Of course. That will be fine." But Nicholas held back as the rest of them turned away to head off. "Wait a minute, though." His hand slipped into Dave's, and squeezed in reassurance or maybe in a plea. "Just between us for now, Father, but I think we're more than friends."

The earl had turned back readily enough, and now he hesitated for less than a blink before saying, "I'm sure we all understood as much, Nicholas, and we're very happy to have David here with us."

"No, I mean …" Those dark blue eyes searched Dave wildly, glowing with a tentatively grasped hope which increased in certainty every moment. "I mean, I think I proposed to David earlier, in the conservatory. Didn't I?" he asked.

"Yes," said David.

"And … I think you accepted me. Didn't you … ?"

"Yes."

"Oh!" Nicholas cried before leaning in to press a kiss against Dave's mouth. "I was hoping it was so."

And then Richard was shaking Dave's hand again, heartily expressing his delight, and welcoming Dave to the family, before gathering his obviously beloved son into his arms and offering congratulations. "You couldn't have made me any happier," the earl said as they all tried to regroup. "Nicholas, this is the last wish I had for you that remained unfulfilled. Until now."

"Thank you, Father."

But there was no way to keep it secret of course. Nicholas and Richard were as damp–eyed as Dave, and Robert couldn't quite suppress his pleased, proud smile. Within ten minutes of them entering the family living room, just about everyone had twigged. And Simon didn't even need to be asked; five minutes later the adults each had a flute of champagne, and the kids had flutes of lemonade. Robin was standing there holding Dave's hand, and gazing devotedly up at him and Nicholas, though he seemed a bit young to really understand what was happening. Given that Dave's other hand held his champagne glass, Nicholas had taken the opportunity to wind an arm about Dave's waist, which was great because Dave feared he was so giddy he might teeter and fall otherwise.

"I don't think Nicholas will mind me acknowledging," the earl said to the gathering, "that I was anxious when he decided to travel to Australia on his own, and planned to spend so much of his time there far beyond our ken. It seemed too bold an enterprise, full of dangers. I was afraid of losing this young man who is so very precious to me. But Nicholas didn't only find his butterflies there. I'm sure those of you who've spent time with him since he returned will agree that he found his own best self. And now, to complete the whole, we discover that he has found a loving partner as well. His future husband. And so I'd like to propose a toast …"

Richard looked across the room to nod to Simon. "Yes, please. Bring everyone in. This is for all the family."

Dave watched as six or seven others filed in, remaining tactfully out of the way, but each with their glass of champagne, and each smiling happily at Nicholas, while considering Dave with an inquisitive friendliness.

"To Nicholas and David," the earl at last said, lifting his glass. "May they enjoy the long and happy life together that they both deserve."

"To Nicholas and David," everyone responded.

And Nicholas leaned in to kiss him again, and Dave gave himself over to it, blushing only with a painful kind of pleasure now. Whooping and cheers, laughter and the clinking of glasses rang in his ears, but that all faded away when Nicholas murmured with his lips brushing Dave's, "You're mine now, you gorgeous darling man."

To which Dave replied, "Yes, I'm all yours."

And it was done.

About Julie Bozza

Ordinary people are extraordinary. We can all aspire to decency, generosity, respect, honesty – and the power of love (all kinds of love!) can help us grow into our best selves.

I write stories about 'ordinary' people finding their answers in themselves and each other. I write about friends and lovers, and the families we create for ourselves. I explore the depth and the meaning, the fun and the possibilities, in 'everyday' experiences and relationships. I believe that embodying these things is how we can live our lives more fully.

Creative works help us each find our own clarity and our own joy. Readers bring their hearts and souls to reading, just as authors bring their hearts and souls to writing – and together we make a whole.

I read books, lots of books, and watch films. I admire art, and love theatre and music. I try to be an awesome partner, sister, daughter, friend. I live an engaged and examined life. And I strive to write as honestly as I can.

I have lived in two countries – England and Australia – which has helped widen my perspective, and I have travelled as well. I love learning, and have completed courses in all kinds of things. My careers have been in Human Resources, and in eLearning and training, so there has always been a focus on my fellow human beings and on understanding, conveying, sharing information.

Knitting gives me some down time and the chance to craft something with my hands. Coffee gives me stimulation and a certain street cred. My favourite colour has segued from pure blue to dark purple, and seems to be segueing again to marine blues.

I think John Keats is the best person who has ever lived.

And that's me! Julie Bozza. Quirky. Queer. Sincere.

If you want to know more, please do come find me at juliebozza.com and libra-tiger.com.

Titles by Julie Bozza

The Butterfly Hunter Trilogy:
     Butterfly Hunter
     Of Dreams and Ceremonies
     Like Leaves to a Tree
     The Thousand Smiles of Nicholas Goring

Albert J. Sterne:
     The Definitive Albert J. Sterne
     Albert J. Sterne: Future Bright, Past Imperfect

Novels and Novellas:
     The Apothecary's Garden
     The Fine Point of His Soul
     Homosapien … a fantasy about pro wrestling
     Mitch Rebecki Gets a Life
     A Night with the Knight of the Burning Pestle
     A Threefold Cord
     The 'True Love' Solution
     The Valley of the Shadow of Death

Stories and Anthologies:
     Call to Arms
     A Certain Persuasion
     An English Heaven
     No Holds Bard
     A Pride of Poppies